Copyright © 2023 by P.C. James and Kathryn Mykel All rights reserved.

No part of this book may be reproduced in any form or by any electronic or mechanical means, including information storage and retrieval systems, without written permission from the author, except for the use of brief quotations in a book review.

Copyright notice: All rights reserved under the International and Pan-American Copyright Conventions. No part of this book may be reproduced or transmitted in any form or by any means, electronic or mechanical, including photocopying and recording, or by any information storage and retrieval system, without permission in writing from publisher. This is a work of fiction. Names, places, characters, and incidents are either the product of the author's imagination or are used fictitiously, and any resemblance to any actual persons, living or dead, organizations, events, or locales is entirely coincidental. Warning: the unauthorized reproduction or distribution of this copyrighted work is illegal. Criminal copyright infringement, including infringement without monetary gain, is investigated by the FBI and is punishable by up to 5 years in prison and a fine of $250,000.

TABLE OF CONTENTS

1. Racket of Intrigue	1
2. Love and Rackets	10
3. Let The Games Begin	19
4. Advantage—Detective	25
5. Courtly Suspicions	34
6. Let The Real Games Begin	41
7. Deuces and Deceptions	49
8. Backhand Whispers	61
9. Game, Set, Mystery	72
10. Doubles Discovery	81
11. Crosscourt Clues	93
12. A Tangled Match	98
13. Serve of Suspicion	110
14. Unseen Backhand	125
15. Netting the Truth	132
16. Volley of Accusations	141
17. The Advantage of Doubt	151
18. The Net Tightens	160
19. Rally for Truth	167
20. A Strong Forehand, Maybe	176
21. Top Spin of Truth	184
22. Netting the Culprit	191
23. Drop Shot	201
24. Championship Clue	211
25. Tennis Court Conclusions	221
Epilogue	224
Duchess of Snodsbury Trilogy	231
Sassy Senior Sleuths	233
About the Author Kathryn Mykel	235
About the Author P.C. James	239

1

RACKET OF INTRIGUE
UPPER WAINBURY, SOMERSET, ENGLAND, JULY 1958

Lady Mary Culpeper, Duchess of Snodsbury, wiped her thumb over a snout-shaped condensation mark on the railway carriage window. Her canine companion, Barkley, stood erect, peering out. The constant chug of the train mixed with pumps of steam and hissing air had heightened her senses, and she buzzed with anticipation. As they approached Upper Wainbury Halt, the station nearest Margie Marmalade's family home, Mary's musings mingled with suspicions of countryside mayhem and the possibility of an escalation to murder.

As the train slowly pulled into the rural stop, Mary spied her three young assistants as well as Margie's mother, her old friend, Nellie Marmalade. All waiting and waving. *The sight of Nellie sure does bring back a fondness—of parties decades past, when we were much younger.* The '20s had been a whirl of gaiety, and even the '30s had their moments until the dark cloud of war had descended. The '40s had been a struggle, and the early '50s were just grim.

Now, pressing toward the '60s, the world was regaining some of its luster. Receiving the Royal Dispatch to groom the debutantes had been the first bright moment in several years. *And all has been well in the months since.* Mary's heart was warmed by this exuberant greeting. Even back home, her Snodsbury estate was regaining its glory, with Mary having risen to the Queen's Commission. *Now a bit of vacation is in order. I shall see if my assistant sleuths have retained their training.*

Margie leapt onto the passenger car and hugged Mary. The other two girls—and even Barkley, at Mary's side—all held their positions, awaiting Mary's exit. Once Margie had released Mary from her clutches, Mary hooked her arm though the handle of her bag, and departed, with the dog shuffling down the steps by her side.

"You should've let Ponsonby come with you today." Dotty Dilliard hummed, her spiral curls bouncing as her head bobbled. Staring past Mary, as if the butler were standing behind, Dotty grinned, and her freckles shifted with her smile. "Then you wouldn't have to carry anything."

It's just a small travel case.

Lady Mary's butler, Ponsonby—a stoic man with old-fashioned notions—was arriving by motorcar with Cook and all their belongings, early this evening. *I pray for the sparring pair of old friends. Let their journey be without incident.*

At the bottom of the steps, Mary planted her feet firmly on the ground letting go of the railing as Berkley weaved around her. *This dog's excitement will trip me up one of these days.*

"Hello, Nellie." Mary opened her free arm to greet her friend with a half hug.

"Welcome to Upper Wainbury, Lady Mary."

Barkley jumped, eager to join the human embrace. "Down, Barkley," Mary commanded.

Barkley heeled and casually approached the other two girls for petting, while they themselves waited to greet Mary.

Nellie stepped back, holding Mary's hand. "I'm so glad you've come. Now that you're here, your sleuthing expertise might set Margie's mind to rest. My daughter's sure that mischief is in the air. Maybe your keen eye will see the facts of the matter."

With a laugh, Mary replied, "It's good to see you again as well, Nellie. And, yes, Margie has filled me with stories of all the strange things happening in your village."

Nellie smiled. "She'll have told you all the evidence to support her wild notions. Be assured, her father and I, and everyone else in the village, don't agree."

"Mother!" Margie cried, bouncing on the pads of her feet. Her honeysuckle yellow locks were straighter than when Mary saw her just months ago, and still not tucked up. "I gave Lady Mary as fair a telling of the events as anyone could. Including why you say there's nothing to bother with."

Nellie shook her head. Her form was an exact duplicate of her daughter's stout frame and soft pink skin, except for Nellie's bouffant hairstyle. Her expression firmly disbelieving, she escorted Mary and the entourage off the platform toward the waiting chauffeured car.

"I'd say Margie's account was very balanced, and she gave her evidence concisely, without any attempt to sway me."

The Pembroke corgi pranced ahead of Mary, his paws skittering over the path as he halted by a stretch of flower beds. Intrigued by a delicate butterfly, he playfully bounded after it with infectious enthusiasm.

Nellie chuckled at the corgi's antics. "Our stationmaster has won awards for best-kept station in the west for several years now. We're very *competitive* around here." She gestured to the vibrant flower beds adorned with lavender, daisies, and dahlias. Baskets filled with pansies and petunias hung overhead as they strolled past—the air fragrant with the mingling scents.

Mary replied with a generous smile. "It's beautifully kept."

The group walked through the small knot of people showing

tickets at the gate. At the car, Nellie continued, "When we get to the manor, and you've freshened up, I can give you the full story. Then you will decide for yourself if there is anything to investigate."

"This tennis party you're hosting," Mary asked. "Will many of the villagers be there? The ones Margie says are involved in the *odd incidents*?" She stepped into the car and waited as the others slid in.

"Yes," Margie replied before her mother could, slipping in next to Mary. "Which is why we need you here. If anything does transpire, it will cast aspersions on the village or our family if it happens on our watch." The young lady of eighteen years flashed a serious glare.

The chauffeur put the car into gear, and the Rolls purred away from the station.

Mary tilted her head. "I understand. But just because something happens in the village, it doesn't mean you or your family will be suspected or accused."

"It does if things point toward my family members," Margie retorted.

Nellie sighed. "That case you all shared in, with the jewel and the phony princess, has Margie seeing mysteries everywhere, and now she thinks her own father is in some way connected." Nellie held up her hand to stop Margie's next outburst. "I'm sorry, my dear, but not everything is a mystery to be solved."

In little time the car turned off the road into the Marmalades' circular driveway, which curved gracefully around flowering bushes.

Mary gazed wistfully at the stately Georgian manor. *Our Snodsbury will soon be returned to its former glory.*

"Things haven't changed here, at all." Mary smiled. "It's just how I remembered it from when we were younger."

An hour later, Mary and Nellie were having afternoon tea on the terrace, while the girls had taken tennis rackets to the court for practice before Sunday's tournament. *It may be all in fun for me, but it's clear by their banter the girls want to win.*

The maid placed the tray on the round cast-iron table between them and exited.

"You see, Mary," Nellie said, "what Margie doesn't understand about the first incident—the deaths of the poor family pets—is that cats and dogs pass on naturally all the time."

"Surely they do, but the cat's passing was suspicious was it not?"

Between sips, Nellie added, "The feline was an outdoor animal that roamed the village all day, every day."

"So, sooner or later it was sure to eat the wrong thing."

Nellie nodded. "It could've been exposed to things like poison put down for rats or mice, or even consumed such a rat or mouse that had itself eaten the poison."

These things do happen, unfortunately, but is Nellie trying to convince me or herself there isn't a bigger problem?

"What about the dog?" Mary asked, realizing Nellie had stopped talking and was stirring a single sugar cube into her teacup.

"Mr. Quartermaine's dog, Abby, was elderly but reported to be in good health. Though it died suddenly, only a week after the cat, old dogs, like old people, often go suddenly."

Barkley grumbled. Sitting at attention in the shade of Mary's chair, his inquisitive gaze following the girls' animated movements on the tennis court.

Even the healthiest of them. "And what is the explanation for the burglary?" Mary prompted. "Surely that is uncommon in a place like Upper Wainbury."

"It's rare, yes," Nellie confirmed. "You must've seen the new road as your train pulled into the station?"

Mary inclined her head. "Very busy, yes. Is it noisy in the evenings?"

"Quite." Nellie added a second sugar cube to her own cup and clanked the spoon against the porcelain before setting it on a napkin. She peered at Mary, who waved her fan. "But more importantly, it means people can be here in no time from the nearby towns. We aren't the secluded oasis we once were."

The new road could bring in undesirables. "There are new residents, I understand." Mary sipped her tea.

Nellie nodded.

"And it was a newcomer's residence that was burgled?" Mary asked.

"Yes. Most of our newcomers are fine folks returning to friends and family in the area. We haven't any newcomers who are the sort to be burglars."

Barkley's ears perked up, and the atmosphere shifted.

Is there really a sort? Anyone could be a culprit of malicious acts. Mary took a satisfying bite of a freshly baked biscuit. *I must commend her cook.*

Nellie hesitated. "The man who was burgled—he's a businessman from London. A nice man, of course, but business people aren't entirely straightforward, are they?"

Are they? I wonder. Seems a good place to start. Mary wiped fallen crumbs from her sundress, and Barkley seized the opportunity, darting his tongue out and lapping the remnants from the patio blocks before Mary raised an objection. "I suspect they wouldn't be good at business if they were." A bemused smile tugged at the corners of Mary's mouth. "Margie says nothing was taken, which is strange for a burglary, don't you agree?"

"As I said, Mr. Beacham, Cyril, is a businessman. He says nothing was taken, but he may have ulterior motives to deny certain possessions were stolen."

"Is that speculation, or do you think he's a crook?" Mary eyed Nellie carefully, judging her response.

"I do speculate, as you say, that perhaps he's hiding his business dealings."

"Margie asserted Constable Watkins also believes nothing was stolen. Is he covering for Cyril?"

Barkley shuffled around her chair. As quickly as he'd stirred, he settled again by her side with his head on his paws.

Overheating, her fan not helping, Mary returned her attention to her friend. Nellie furrowed her brow. "I'm sure he's just repeating what Cyril told him. Constable Watkins is a nice man, but he doesn't want county detectives down here bossing him about any more than Cyril wants people snooping into his business affairs."

"Well, what exactly is Cyril Beacham's business?"

A bead of sweat ran down Nellie's temple as she looked on fondly at the girls on the court, and then back to Mary. "He has an art and antique gallery in London."

"He can't travel to London *every day* from *here*, surely?"

"No. Cyril claims his junior partner runs the gallery. While he flits about the country and the continent searching for items to sell." She waved her hand around. "He's often away for a week or more, so he travels *somewhere*."

While Mary contemplated the narrative, Nellie sipped her tea.

"You say 'he claimed.' Don't you believe him?"

Nellie fidgeted in her chair, and was slow to answer. "He's a nice enough man, but people in the art and antiques trade are generally considered, shall we say, less than honest. The truth is, I just really don't trust him."

In my experience, no one trusts such dealers. Mary tilted her head. "Have you been to his gallery?"

"Good heavens, no." Nellie set her teacup down with a clatter. "I don't know anything about art or antiques. I'd be sold a fake and be none the wiser."

"And Cyril's house?"

A gentle breeze blew, and Nellie tucked a few stray hairs back into her net whimsy. Her dark beige blouse was doing a better job at hiding her perspiration than Mary's summer dress was. "He does have a lot of antiques and artwork in his home. I'm surprised nothing was stolen. That's why I have suspicions about his claim."

"So, you're suspicious about this burglary, but not about the sequence of strange happenings?" Mary asked as Nellie fanned herself with her hand and the girls bantered on the court. The heat, the conversation, and the practice game all intensified.

"Correct. Each individual event may be a little peculiar if you're looking for something from nothing, but there's no connection."

Barkley huffed, and Mary agreed, "The events might be considered an escalation."

"I don't believe there's anything more serious to come," Nellie replied dismissively.

"What about your husband, Gerry, losing his keys?" *If I recall correctly, he's an older man, at least ten years Nellie's senior, whose principal interest is fox hunting.*

Nellie shook her head. "My husband has become very forgetful of late. It isn't just the keys. He's mislaid other things also."

Barkley waddled to a ceramic dish better suited for a hound than a corgi—labeled DOG on the side. "But you must see *why* Margie is worried. After all these village events, things start happening in her own family."

"Coincidence. Besides, Margie is mostly away at school," Nellie replied. "She doesn't realize how absentminded her father is becoming, and she believes him when he claims his own things have been *stolen*. Of course, he doesn't tell her when the missing items turn up."

Found where he undoubtedly left them. Aging is the simplest explanation here.

Nellie grimaced and faced Barkley, who lapped at the water, splashing it everywhere. "I'm growing quite worried about Gerry, actually. But it's completely unrelated, you see."

"I do." Mary nodded thoughtfully. "While you may think Margie's concerns aren't up to snuff, I still feel there's something in them. Despite her jovial manner, your daughter has a keen mind. Don't underestimate her."

Mary wasn't positive if her friend's responding laugh was regarding her daughter or the case as Mary perceived it, until Nellie replied, "Then you have a week to find out what that 'something' is."

Mary smiled grimly. "I'll begin at once in the hope of getting to the bottom of it all. You may not believe there's something behind these events, and I don't yet know what 'it' is, but it's there." Barkley woofed, and Mary added, "I feel it in my bones."

2

LOVE AND RACKETS

Later that evening, Lady Mary had sufficiently cooled off from her time in the hot summer sun. She stepped out of the grand manor onto the gravel driveway, greeted by the twitter of birds chirping and the fragrance of purple phlox. A haze hung in the air, casting an ethereal glow over the countryside estate. She waited for her staff, and her vintage Rolls-Royce approached, coming to a stop right in front of her.

Maybe I should purchase a newer vehicle? The royal commission provided me with welcome funds. She gazed longingly at her husband's vintage car. *Ponsonby would be equally unhappy at losing the connection.* The faithful butler had served with her late husband in the army before taking up service as the butler and valet.

Ponsonby, now *her* reliable butler and friend, stepped out from behind the wheel, his impeccable attire unmarred by the long journey. Lady Mary admired his astute nature—a quality that had served her well for many years.

Cook, a rotund woman with wild, curly red hair that threatened to escape the confines of her frilly white cap, clambered out of the car clutching a picnic basket, with a stack of recipe books precariously balanced atop the lid, and shoved it all into Ponsonby's arms. Barkley positioned himself at Mary's feet. Undisturbed by Cook's frantic motions, he fixed his watchful gaze on Mary. The dog was an ever-present guardian of her comfort, and company.

Lady Mary raised a fleeting hand to check her own perfectly coiffed hair. She shook her head. *Silly. I've better things to do than become absorbed in fretting over appearances.* She glanced at Ponsonby, who inclined his head respectfully but with something approaching a wry grin on his face. Cook bent back into the vehicle. Then, echoing her enthusiasm, her hurried footsteps on the gravel, along with Cook's energy—her trademark—was accompanied by a symphony of clattering pans.

Mary greeted her faithful chef. "Good evening, Cook."

"Oh, milady! Just wait until I tell you about the delightful meals I've planned!"

"I have no doubt your culinary skills would impress us all, Cook. But Mrs. Marmalade has a cook, a Mrs. Jenkins, as I already assured you. You should just enjoy the visit, as we all will."

"Well, I can't just sit on my derriere for the weekend." Cook huffed and adjusted her cap. She eyed Barkley, and Lady Mary exchanged glances with Ponsonby. "He's been fed too. Not to worry."

"I expected you several hours earlier—is everything all right?" Mary asked Ponsonby, rallying the conversation.

"Just a spot of trouble with a tire, ma'am. Not to worry." Another wry grin peeked out before he composed himself.

"Very well. Let us see you both, and the luggage, inside. Mrs. Marmalade's other guests will be arriving in the morning." With an obedient trot, Barkley followed Cook, his royal-corgi demeanor radiating quiet obedience. They all enjoyed a fine dinner prepared by the cooks, and lively conversation got them caught up on the past years. Ponsonby excused himself, relaying his plans to stop by the local pub. And the rest of the group retired for the evening.

THE NEXT MORNING, Mary assumed her position between Nellie and the trio of young sleuths—Margie, Winnie, and Dotty—in the grand foyer of the hall to greet the other guests.

The first to arrive was Cyril Beacham—a businessman and art dealer, accompanied by his wife, Frances. They stepped into the foyer with an air of city sophistication. Lady Mary had already received her fill of details about the man from Nellie.

"Cyril, Frances, welcome," Nellie greeted them warmly. "Allow me to introduce you to Mary, Her Grace, the Duchess of Snodsbury—a dear friend of ours."

Cyril Beacham, tall and distinguished, proffered a long, thin hand toward Lady Mary. "A pleasure to meet you, Lady Mary. I've heard much about your impeccable taste and keen eye for art."

Lady Mary quickly affixed a smile, unsure who had given him that impression, but acknowledging the compliment. "The pleasure is mine, Cyril. I look forward to exploring your world of art during our stay here."

And I'll be keeping an eye on you. You're too much the man of the world for my taste and, for all your sophistication, there's something of the night in you.

Mary greeted Cyril's wife, an equally slender woman with perfectly pin-curled chestnut hair and sparkling hazel eyes. "Pleasure to meet you, Frances."

"Please, Lady Mary, call me Fran," she replied, annunciating the *N* of her name in a dry drawl.

Barkley's paws skittered lightly across the polished parquet flooring, and he came to a stop right at Fran's feet. Mary's breath caught in her throat, uncertain how the poised woman would react to the presence of the furry canine. A small, tentative bark escaped Barkley's tiny mouth, and all eyes were on Fran as she extended her graceful arm, gently nudging his chin, prompting him to move away.

Suppressing her chagrin, Mary composed a smile as Barkley returned to her side, his head held high despite the subtle snub.

Next to arrive, only moments later, were the Illingsworths, Mrs. Marmalade's neighbors.

"Lady Mary, may I present Mr. and Mrs. Illingsworth and their daughter Vanessa," Nellie introduced them. Victor was a plump gentleman with a sharp wit, who, according to Nellie, had made a name for himself in the legal profession, while Roseanne possessed a sweetness and charm that was hard to resist.

Vanessa—a gangly, sporty-looking girl—curtsied, before stepping aside to chat with the girls.

Victor Illingsworth outstretched a chunky hand toward Mary, a mischievous glimmer in his eyes. "A pleasure to meet you, Lady Mary. I hope your stay at this fine estate brings about intriguing conversations and perhaps a touch of mystery." He winked, and his wife jabbed him playfully on the arm.

Mary chuckled. "Indeed, Mr. Illingsworth. With a group as fascinating as this, I have no doubt our stay will be filled with both."

She glanced over at the three young sleuths—Margie, a softness about her pink complexion in contrast to her jerky movements; Winnie, the clear leader of the pack, head and shoulders taller than her counterparts, and her stern expression accentuated by her razor-sharp straight black hair; and Dotty, her frizzy hair and lazy eye both distractions from her keen observational skills. Mary observed the girls had now turned their attention away from the newly arrived guests.

"Lady Mary." Roseanne Illingsworth greeted her. "Excuse my husband's flirtatious behavior. He does it on purpose to annoy me." She reached out a manicured hand covered in too many rings. Her cheeks were pink, and she flashed Mary a genuine smile. "It's a pleasure to meet you. The girls have told me all about your perilous escapades during their coming-out."

They shook hands, but before Mary could respond that it wasn't Roseanne's husband she'd been thinking of when she looked so disapproving, Roseanne had already turned to Nellie, and air-kissed her on both cheeks. "I do apologize for our late arrival; we had some car trouble."

"Oh my," Mary interjected, and Roseanne's attention refocused on Mary. "You weren't the only ones. My butler, Ponsonby, drove over a nail, which resulted in a flat tire."

"Well, that is curious indeed," Victor replied, returning his attention to Mary.

"See, Mum, I told you. Strange things are happening all over the countryside," Margie chirped, glaring around Mary at her mother.

"Cars break down and tires pop all the time, Margie. Stop jumping to conclusions," Nellie scolded. "Please, everyone, follow me out onto the terrace for drinks." Her cook and maid materialized at that precise moment. "Oh, do tell the cook if you have any food preferences she should be aware of."

Nellie walked out of the room, and Beacham approached the cook, speaking in a tone too low for Mary to hear. Barkley woofed, following the girls as their squealing voices trailed out onto the patio. Mary also followed, still thinking about the arrivals and her assistant sleuths.

I'll need to find an appropriate time to clue them in on the updates from Nellie. They'll need to keep a watchful eye as well.

Nellie ushered the group outside, where the staff had been busy during the Marmalades' introductions, laying out a spread of confections, glasses of champagne and Pimms. The smell of gillyflowers, crowded in flower beds along the wall, filled the morning air.

Armed with her slightly outdated cloche hat, Mary took a seat under the shade of a nearby sycamore. Victor and Roseanne sat on either side of her. Barkley chose his seat under the table next to Fran.

Cyril chuckled. "Funny how dogs can sense those who do and don't like them."

But he usually chooses men, so why didn't he take to you, Mr. Beacham? Mary watched Margie, Winnie, Dotty and Vanessa run off back to the tennis court, under the clear blue sky. Nellie had given them the nod that the need for proper etiquette was concluded for the time being.

"Ah, Gerry, there you are, my dear," Nellie called affectionately to her husband, who looked flustered at his own entrance to the party.

Collecting himself, Gerry greeted his guests as the maid brought him a refreshing drink. "My apologies for arriving late. We had a bit of car trouble. Fortunately it was nothing the driver couldn't handle."

Mary flashed a sidelong look to Nellie. *Three car incidents in two days surely isn't a coincidence. Curious indeed.*

"Let's walk the gardens, shall we?" Nellie prompted. "Before the tennis matches start."

Mary nodded, and the ladies gathered. While exploring the grounds and surrounding gardens, Mary chewed on the incidents as Margie had relayed them, recalling Nellie's contrasting account and adding the multiple car problems experienced just yesterday and today. Mary was cataloging the case.

They passed a bed of Piccadilly shrubs—a hybrid tea-blend

rose of orange and pink coloring—nearly three feet tall. Mary was instantly homesick for the sprawling gardens of her own Snodsbury estate. The new gardener had recently wooed her with delight over a special new rose variety called *Super Star*. She dreamt of returning to a perfectly cultivated wonderland when this visit was over. *Home.*

Nellie brought the group to a halt at the tennis court, transitioning from the fleeting beauty of the gardens to the upcoming activity. "Are you all ready for our Marmalade Family Annual Tennis Tournament?"

Her query about the tournament was met with a collective murmur of agreement.

"As ready as I'll ever be." Roseanne beamed. "But you know what my husband is like—he has to win at everything he does, and the other men aren't any less competitive."

The other two wives chuckled at this remark. "Maybe Lady Mary's presence might restrain their competitive nature."

"I hope so." Nellie laughed.

Fran Beacham shook her head. "Nothing stops Cyril when his mind is set."

As the group continued their leisurely stroll, Nellie filled Mary in on the plans for the tournament. "We usually pick the couples who will play the first match at about eleven." She checked her watch. "Which is soon. We'll stop for lunch after a match or two, then carry on with our tennis. It's a rather long but fun day."

Just as Nellie finished speaking, a mischievous rustling in the bushes caught Mary's attention. Out of the foliage bounded Barkley, his ears flopping and his tongue hanging out.

In a comical twist, Barkley had taken Nellie's words as a cue for action. He darted toward a tennis ball carelessly left on the pathway, his little legs pumping. Mary and the others turned their attention to him, and he scooped up the ball triumphantly in his mouth.

The ladies giggled, but Fran ignored the friendly pup, asking, "Will other neighbors be playing this year? Other than us, I mean."

"No, after last year, we thought it best to invite only those who could behave themselves." Nellie winked. "The pool escapades are too fresh in our minds."

"I hardly dare ask," Mary said, rejoining Nellie, holding her grin at imagining what story might unfold. "What happened at the pool?"

Nellie shuddered. "Some of the younger people, not our children . . ." She paused. "Well, let's just say, the *mishaps* at the pool involved tipsy participants who lost their clothes." Nellie's account was delivered with amusement and feigned propriety.

"Shocking," Mary said jokingly. However, as Fran and Nellie's expressions turned serious, it was clear the incident had left its mark on the group, even causing a measure of discomfort.

"You may think we're all prudish, Mary," Fran said, "but this was less than pleasing. Nellie has described it far too delicately for you to truly understand."

Mary changed the subject. "Have I a partner? It's mixed doubles, isn't it?"

"You can have Cyril," Fran said. "I'm sure he would be happy to step in to fill the lack of partners, and I'd be happy to sit the game out."

"Our vicar, Reverend Sexton, is a good tennis player and was planning to join us today," Nellie said. "Did I forget to mention it, Mary? The day before you arrived he came down with a bit of a bug. Choose one of the girls to partner with. Any one of the four certainly has the energy to play twice."

Mary stopped to observe a winding pathway lined with drifts of perennials—a vision like a beautiful watercolor painting.

"Maybe it's best I just stay here and watch," Mary replied. "I haven't played in many years, and I'm just as happy to enjoy the scenery as to play tennis." She smiled to soften her refusal, but her mind ran on . . .

And I want to watch you all without the distraction of chasing a tennis ball. If Margie is right, and I fear she is, then something will happen soon, and what better place than at a party?

3

LET THE GAMES BEGIN

Lady Mary stifled a sigh-turned-yawn, covering her mouth with her fan. Just before lunch, the sun was already blazing her skin hot with its full-on rays as she sat in an old deck chair. *I shouldn't be yawning.*

Fran Beacham's observation about her husband, Cyril, had proven accurate: he detested losing. Despite his polished and refined appearance, Cyril was a whirlwind of energy, determinedly battling to salvage every shot as he darted across the court. On the opposite side, the Illingsworths steadily fell behind.

Long ago, Mary had viewed Fred Perry winning at Wimbledon and in Paris, with her husband and their vibrant circle of friends. Yawning was far from her mind back then; the days and nights had overflowed with vitality, laughter, and camaraderie, a distant era when she was a youthful reflection of the matron she'd become. The present day found her in the midst of a crowd she hardly knew, sweltering under the scorching sun. Boredom gnawed at her, and a feeling of insignificance had crept in. The weight of years was suddenly palpable, and the vitality that had once coursed through her had waned. She shook herself free from the grip of despondency.

"Nonsense and silliness," she whispered. *I still have lots of life in me.*

The game ended as Mary had suspected it would, with the Beachams as victors. Someone who wants to win will always beat those who only want to play. The two couples came off the court, shaking hands and chatting amicably, and were replaced by Dotty, Margie, Winnie and Vanessa. Mary grinned. *These girls will be a challenge for Beacham that even his exertions may not overcome.*

Despite Cyril Beacham's friendly banter earlier in the day, he sat as far from Mary as the seating allowed. She pondered whether Nellie's suggestion he was not quite honest was in fact correct. *Is he taking no chance of giving himself away by sitting next to me?*

The two couples poured themselves large tumblers of lemonade. She shouldn't have been surprised to witness Cyril add something to his glass from a hip flask pulled from his navy blue blazer draped over the chairback.

"Are you too warm, Mary?" Nellie approached Mary, who was fanning herself vigorously. "Gerry could move your chair into the shade."

"It is rather hot," Mary agreed. Even in her lightest flower-patterned sundress, she was sweating. "Perhaps I should move under that tree again." She pointed her fan toward the sycamore, which stood closer to the tennis court.

Short-staffed without a butler, Nellie called her husband to Mary's aid, and between Gerry and her ladyship they carried the chair and a small table for Mary to set her drink on.

"That's much better, thank you," Mary said to Gerry as she settled once more into the deck chair to watch the new game. Vanessa and Margie were racking up winning scores.

Cyril Beacham eyed the young players with an intensity only a win-at-any-cost personality would warrant.

Or was it the young girls in their short white tennis dresses that drew his gaze? Mary mused unhappily. *It must be very tiring to have Cyril as a husband.*

Mary's decision to move had been as much strategic as it was for comfort. From her new vantage point, she had the game and all the guests within her sightline. The Illingsworths, Fran Beacham, and her host and hostess were in a lively, laughing conversation—pipe smoke puffing and drinks now flowing.

Ponsonby approached with another glass of water, and Mary put down her fan. "What do you think?" She discreetly gestured toward the raucous group.

"I fear, my lady, the level of play won't improve as the afternoon arrives."

Mary laughed. "And the finals later will be even worse."

"Quite so."

"However, my question wasn't just about tennis," Mary added.

"The locals in the pub last night were scathing about Mr. Beacham. He's not well liked, and he's conspicuously silent during today's conversations," Ponsonby remarked.

Mary accepted his observations with a nod. "I think in this case, it's he who has set himself apart."

"His gaze is certainly fixed on the trophy," Ponsonby replied.

Before Mary could formulate a response, a gasp escaped her lips. Barkley, attuned to her emotions, whined softly. Cyril Beacham—dressed in his sharply creased sporting khaki shorts and white shirt—slumped sideways in his chair. Mary was all too familiar with that posture—an eerie mimicry of a lifeless figure. Cyril twisted in an unnatural way, and as his form settled, the once-friendly chatter of the group faded to stunned stillness at the unexpected turn of events.

Ponsonby sprang into action with purposeful efficiency as he dashed across the lawn.

Mary also sprang from her seat and trailed closely behind Ponsonby. Barkley accompanied her. The trio arrived at Beacham's side before the others could come out of their stupor.

Ponsonby's experienced hands moved with a precision only years of service could cultivate. He knelt beside Cyril's body and searched for a pulse at both wrist and neck. Mary stood beside Ponsonby, her heart racing—a solemn shake of his head expressed to Mary exactly what she'd expected.

"Phone the police," Mary said urgently to Ponsonby. Nellie Marmalade's alarmed cry pierced the air, and her guests' eyes widened as everyone approached Ponsonby and Mary standing beside the still figure of Cyril Beacham.

"What's happening?" Nellie trembled, spilling her drink.

Mary sternly addressed the query head-on. "Cyril Beacham is dead." She gazed up at the ring of faces surrounding her and the body.

Gerry's response was tinged with skepticism. "Natural causes, no doubt. A heart attack. Heaven knows he's done enough to bring one on. We were all just saying so, watching him play earlier." He chuckled cynically, puffing his pipe.

Mary, however, remained resolute. It was too soon for a simple explanation—an easy conclusion. "I fear foul play, Gerry. There are none of the usual heart attack signs. We must summon the police."

Mary's gaze caught Fran Beacham, staring with a disconcerting stillness, entranced by Cyril's lifeless body, her face emotionless.

Dream or nightmare?

The girls were quick to put down their racquets and rush to Mary's side. The group's horror morphed into a collective dilemma as Nellie voiced a practical concern, her features etched with horror. "What shall we do in the meantime? We can't leave him here to bake in the hot sun."

A morbid thought, but a necessary consideration.

"We must," Mary replied firmly. "And nothing must be touched. Including the drinks. Whatever killed him might still be lingering."

"He had his own hip flask," Fran offered.

"I noticed that." Mary's gaze fixed on Fran, who was bending, hand outstretched, as if to check her husband's pulse. "Please don't touch anything. We don't want to destroy evidence."

Ponsonby reappeared on the scene. His dignified strides carried him across the lawn, his commitment to his duties evident even in the midst of turmoil. "The police are on their way, my lady. Constable Watkins will be here just as soon as he's alerted the county Criminal Investigation Department. I suggested he come through the gate, directly to the tennis court area."

The wheels were set in motion, and everyone's expressions showed that the promise of outside expertise was both reassuring and unsettling.

Sensing the discomfort in the ranks, Mary took charge, her decision motivated by practicality and compassion. "Let's retire." She ushered everyone toward the house. Barkley remained steadfast by the body. Mary snapped her fingers, and he followed the others—taking up his sentry duty to protect the guests instead.

"I'll stay with the—" Gerry began. "Someone from the household should be here when—"

"Ponsonby and I will stay as well," Mary said swiftly.

Gerry snorted dismissively with his pipe clenched between his teeth. "His death is a coincidence. We're not responsible," he muttered.

"I never suggested you were," Mary emphasized. "However, you're the *hosts*, and this *is* your house and grounds."

"Cyril always overdid himself. That's what it'll turn out to be, you'll see." Gerry waved his hand toward the dead man.

The three stood guard as Nellie guided the others away.

It's time for my young sleuths to spring into action. Mary dispassionately watched Gerry, who blew out a puff of smoke. His expressions fluttering between disbelief, puzzlement, and . . . relief?

4

ADVANTAGE—DETECTIVE

Constable Watkins arrived a short time later. He communicated the news they had been waiting for: "Detectives are on their way." He proceeded to the task at hand—questioning the individuals present.

"Look here, Watkins," Gerry blustered. "We should wait for those detectives, or we'll have to repeat ourselves."

Watkins responded with poised resolve. "That may be, sir, but I have *my* job to do." His professional stance pleased Mary.

Gerry sighed and explained the events that had transpired, his explanation mirroring the confusion that had been on his face since Cyril's death. Watkins's furrowed brow betrayed his perplexity with Gerry, who couldn't explain the man's demise with any certainty, even though he'd witnessed the occurrence.

Unsure if Gerry's difficulty was concern for his home, or pride, or if there was more to it, Mary interrupted Gerry's confused statements. "Constable, I was seated in a position that afforded the best view of the events leading up to Cyril's collapse. Perhaps I can help. I was sitting over there." She gestured to her chair under the tree.

"Very well, ma'am," Watkins replied, his tone respectful. "Perhaps we could start with your name."

Mary obliged by providing him with enough context to establish her credibility as a reliable witness. "I am Mary Culpeper, Duchess of Snodsbury, and a skilled amateur sleuth." The constable didn't respond, instead he continued to scribe her title into his notepad without glancing up. Hoping to make him understand the importance of her assistance with the investigation, she composed her demeanor and recounted the sparse details of the last few minutes leading up to Cyril Beacham's demise.

"I recommend you speak to Ponsonby next." She referred Watkins to her butler with a gesture, and Ponsonby provided his recounting, similar to Mary's, with a precision that left no room for doubt of his competence either.

Mary was familiar enough with Ponsonby's ways to detect a subtle undercurrent of disapproval as he interacted with Constable Watkins. *I suspect Watkins's lack of recognition of my title has contributed to Ponsonby's apparent less-than-favorable opinion of the constable. I'm not offended, but my supporters are not so tolerant.* She smirked.

The scene was interrupted by the arrival of a group of police officers in uniform and two men in suits. Their sudden appearance marked a new phase in the investigation, and the atmosphere shifted as all eyes turned toward the newcomers. The men proceeded across the lawn to join the small group around the body, and acknowledged Constable Watkins with a slight nod.

One of the suited men addressed Gerry directly, his question simple and straightforward. "Are you the homeowner?"

Gerry stepped forward. "I am. Gerry Marmalade." He offered a handshake, a clear sign both of greeting and his willingness to collaborate.

The officer ignored Gerry's offered hand, signaling an equally clear delineation of roles.

To Watkins the officer commanded, "You go and help the others isolate the crime scene."

Watkins, dutifully slipping his notebook into his pocket, hastened to comply, leaving the tennis area to join the others.

As the officer's attention turned to Mary, his tone remained brisk and businesslike. "And you are?"

The directness of his question prompted Mary to make a quick decision. With a cold edge to her tone, she pulled rank. "Mary Culpeper, Duchess of Snodsbury."

The officer's reaction was subtle but telling. His momentary hesitation betrayed his surprise, an indication he hadn't been fully prepared for the presence of witnesses with such influence here.

"I see," he responded with a note of respect, then turned to Ponsonby. His query, meant to ascertain Ponsonby's role, held a hint of wry humor. "And you? Are you Duke of somewhere?"

Ponsonby's response was laced with his customary reserve, if not with a subtle rebuff. "No," Ponsonby replied icily. "I'm Her Grace's butler, Ponsonby."

As the exchange unfolded, the veranda bore witness to a clash of social dynamics and a dance of authority.

"Well, I'm Detective Inspector John Acton, and I'm in charge of this case. Nobody leaves," he asserted, his gaze shifting toward Mary, "unless I say they can."

His implication is clear enough—the investigation is now under his control, and any potential suspects, or witnesses, will remain within his jurisdiction until he deems otherwise . . . Or until we start our own investigation. Again, Mary smiled.

He gestured toward his associate. "This is Detective Sergeant Reynolds, and he will begin taking your statements while I examine the body."

Acton turned away and knelt beside Cyril, still slumped in the deck chair. The three witnesses, who'd been guarding the body, now directed their attention at Sergeant Reynolds.

Reynolds's approach was less authoritative, and his suggestion reflected a consideration for Mary's comfort. "Maybe, Lady Mary, I could start with you, and then you can return to the shade of the house."

Mary was inclined to take offense at the assumption she was too weak to stand outside but bit her tongue. "We can all stand in the shade of that sycamore." She gestured to the tree she'd been seated under. "It's where I was sitting, so you'll see from my vantage point while I explain."

"If the two gentlemen would wait here," Reynolds said. "It's best you give your statements as you remember them and not be influenced by others."

Mary and Reynolds walked the short distance back to her seat. She pointed across the lawn toward Cyril. "As you see, I had a good view of everything."

His gaze followed hers to where Acton was still crouched, staring at Cyril's body.

Mary quickly recounted the day.

"And that's everything?" Reynolds asked.

"Everything that happened today," Mary replied. "But you should know strange things have been happening around Cyril Beacham and the village lately."

Reynolds arched an eyebrow. "Such as?"

"It's not my story to tell," Mary said. "I don't live in the village. Nellie Marmalade and her daughter Margie should give you the full story, but the man's house was burgled, and there's been a spate of problems with cars."

"Thank you. I'll see what the others can add." They both walked back to Gerry and Ponsonby.

"I think I'll stay out here but sit in the shade again," Mary said to Reynolds. "But, Ponsonby, please ensure no one interferes with Cyril's hip flask before the police have it properly recorded."

"Very well, my lady." Ponsonby watched Acton intently, though the inspector was very correctly avoiding touching the body or Cyril's clothes.

"I'll see that the hip flask is properly recorded so its contents can be analyzed." Reynolds grinned. "Now, gentlemen," he continued as Mary went back to her seat in the shade, "which of you wants to start?"

"I will," Gerry said. "My wife will be wondering what is happening out here, and the sooner I can tell her, the better it will be."

Gerry gave his statement in brisk tones, emphasizing his belief this investigation wasn't warranted. "Cyril was a middle-aged man who drank too much. In the heat, and with his tearing around the court like a madman, he overexerted himself and paid the price."

When Reynolds had dismissed Gerry, he called for Ponsonby, who approached quickly. "Have you anything to add?"

"I saw nothing of the events leading up to Mr. Beacham's death and only became aware of it when I noticed Lady Mary witnessing it. I was handing her the cold drink and had my back to the others, you see."

"Was there anything you saw earlier that might be significant?"

"Nothing. The guests arrived, were admitted to the house and greeted by the Marmalades. I'm here to cater to Lady Mary's needs, not to take part in the running of this house."

"Then, if you've nothing to add," Reynolds said, "you may wish to return to the house as well."

"Lady Mary asked me to see the police treat Mr. Beacham's

hip flask with the importance it deserves," Ponsonby replied. "And until I see that, I'll remain here."

Reynolds chuckled and gestured to the men just arriving. "Our forensic team is here. You shouldn't have long to wait."

Mary silently observed from her seat. The men quickly ran through their tasks, and the hip flask was bagged as evidence.

"You're still here?" Acton asked Ponsonby, moving nearer to Reynolds as the team worked around the body.

"I've carried out my watch as instructed," Ponsonby replied, and left the two detectives to their discussion; then he went to Lady Mary and confirmed the forensic officers had bagged the hip flask.

"And we have been dismissed," he added to his confirmation.

Mary laughed. "We'll no doubt have some interesting discussions with Inspector Acton over the coming days."

"I fear he won't welcome our assistance," Ponsonby agreed.

Ponsonby escorted Mary inside the house, and she found her way to the drawing room, where the others were gathered. She signaled Margie, Dotty, and Winnie to leave the other group and join her in the farthest corner of the room.

"Did any of you see what happened to Mr. Beacham?" Mary asked when they were surrounding her.

Dotty's frizzy ginger curls bounced as she shook her head. Winnie noted, "We had our backs to Mr. Beacham."

"I did," Margie commented to Mary. "When Dotty was winding up to serve, I saw Mr. Beacham slump in his chair. Earlier, I also saw him take what looked like a flask from his jacket and pour something into his own glass."

"I saw that too. Anything else?"

Dotty said, "Vanessa was just telling us he, Mr. Beacham, pulled a strange face after he'd drunk from his glass."

Margie shook her head. "I didn't see that because I was expecting Dotty to serve and I was focused on her."

"So we'll speculate he might've been poisoned," Mary muttered. "Ponsonby and I stayed watching until the police forensic staff secured the evidence."

"This will look bad for my family." Margie flopped down into a wingback chair. "It's happening here on our property, I mean. If Fran Beacham wanted to poison him, and I wouldn't blame her if she did"—she glanced up at the group and quickly diverted her attention to a stray thread on her shorts—"she could have done it anywhere and anytime. This makes it look like our party was to blame."

"You didn't like Mr. Beacham?" Mary asked.

Margie shook her head. "He had a reputation for not keeping his hands to himself."

"What?" Winnie cried, she and Dotty looking aghast.

"Not with me, dummy." Margie blushed. "I'm just telling you what I've heard."

"If you tell this to the police"—Mary stared at Margie—"they'll certainly have another motive to consider."

Margie grimaced. "But with my family being the most likely suspects. Like you, they'll think the worst."

"Or it could have been Mr. and Mrs. Illingsworth," Winnie offered as an afterthought. "They were here and could have wanted your parents to take the blame."

As they were still deep in conversation, Cook bustled into the room, a platter of freshly baked scones in hand. Her voice was as lively as ever. "Ladies, please do try these scones. Fresh out of the oven, they are. Perfect with a spot of tea, I promise!"

Margie took a scone with a distracted smile, still mulling over the discussion. "That doesn't help," she finally replied to the alternative suggestion Winnie had supplied before Cook arrived.

Mary grew somber. "I don't like keeping things from the police, but in this case I think you should let this side of Mr.

Beacham's character be exposed by an adult. You can corroborate it, if asked."

Cook waited on the others to take scones and then she exited the room.

"You think it's something to do with his business dealings, Lady Mary?" Dotty asked.

"I would prefer the police to delve further into it."

"But we can't ignore it as a motive," Winnie said. "If he was *that kind of man*, there could be many local people who had it in for him."

"But they weren't here today," Mary objected.

"His hip flask could have been tampered with elsewhere," Winnie pointed out. "I imagine many people knew him well enough to know he carried it."

Mary puzzled over the speculation for a moment. "It isn't strong, but I agree we must keep it in mind."

Margie, Dotty and Winnie promptly began speaking at once, each giving their opinion.

Mary held up her hand to quell the noise. "It seems we're divided on that question. No matter, we'll know soon enough, I'm sure."

She turned to Ponsonby, who'd joined them. "I have a task for you, old friend."

"And what is that, my lady?" he asked.

"Will you take yourself off to the village pub, and find out what you can about the victim?"

"Of course," Ponsonby replied. "What about the other players in our court?"

"Oh, and ask about our police officers, Acton, Reynolds, and Watkins as well."

Ponsonby flashed a puzzled expression. "Why do you think the authorities are unreliable?"

"I don't know," Mary replied. "But I do know strange things have been happening around Mr. Beacham for some time." She raised her eyebrows. "It may well be that a local person is to blame, and one of the investigators could very well be that person."

5

COURTLY SUSPICIONS

Standing in the Marmalades' foyer close to her staff and the young ladies, Mary asked Ponsonby, "Did you learn anything in the pub last night? About our tennis couples."

"I learned Beacham was standoffish, so the locals say. Mr. Beacham had never frequented the White Horse Pub, and that is a mark against any newcomer."

"I fear the White Horse could be too rural for the likes of Cyril Beacham. Talk of sheep and turnips probably wouldn't interest him at all."

Ponsonby tempered a smile. Only the faintest quivering of his lips suggested he agreed. "No, my lady, and no one in the pub would be likely to buy any art or antiques, I should imagine. There was nothing in common between him and the locals. However, no one knew of any actual wrongdoing. Several even acknowledged he was civil when they'd met him."

Mary frowned. "I'd hoped we might have learned about the occurrences in the village. Whether they were pranks or practical jokes, for instance."

"I would have to live here for a hundred years before they would share something like that with me," Ponsonby said. "The locals still think the Marmalades are newcomers, and I believe they've been here for decades."

"That's true," Margie agreed ruefully. "I was born and grew up here, and I'm still a visitor to the older folks."

"It's the way of quiet villages," Mary agreed, "but I'd still hoped someone might let something slip." Mary eyed Ponsonby wondering if there might be a story he was failing to share in front of the girls.

He gave her no indication of anything salacious but continued with the recounting of his investigative efforts. "The landlord did say he heard a motorbike on the night of the robbery at the Beacham house. And believed the burglar came by way of the new road."

Mary's brow furrowed as she posed her question, her gaze fixed on Margie. "Are there any people with motorbikes in the vicinity?"

"Several young men have them," Margie replied thoughtfully, her fingers tapping gently on her chin. "And Miss Tilley, the village school teacher, has one as well." Her lips quirked and her expression was a mix of amusement and skepticism. "I don't see any of them being interested in Mr. Beacham's art or antiques." Her lips curled further into a half smile, as if she was amused by the absurdity. "Even Miss Tilley wouldn't know where to sell anything she stole. None of them would have the connections for art theft, if you see what I mean?"

Mary's thoughts aligned with Margie's assessment, and Ponsonby's nod made his understanding evident.

The conversation carried the weight of implication—that while the locals might own motorbikes, their lack of connections and motive made them unlikely suspects in the case.

Ponsonby contributed his own insights as he, Mary and the sleuths moved to the sitting room joining the rest of the group. "There was discussion about locals who owned bikes when the landlord recounted it. But he was positive it didn't sound like any of the local ones—claiming it as a machine with a much bigger engine."

Inspector Acton and Sergeant Reynolds strode purposefully into the room, their entrance commanding the attention of everyone present. The grave expressions of the two police officers confirmed Mary's suspicions of foul play.

"Well, Inspector"—Fran Beacham's voice cut through the air with a mixture of anticipation and anxiety—"was it a heart attack?"

The question hung heavy in the air and Acton's response was deliberate, his words chosen with care as he addressed the gathering. "The police doctor thinks not, madam. He'll know better after the postmortem, but he thinks your husband was poisoned." His teaser of the medical assessment left the room in a hushed tension.

"You did this!" Fran screamed, fixing her gaze and pointing her finger at Victor Illingsworth. "Inspector, arrest this man!" Fran's accusation was like a sudden gust of wind.

Illingsworth's face flushed with anger, his features contorted as he faced Fran head-on. "If anyone poisoned him, it was you! Poison is a woman's weapon, after all."

Acton's voice boomed like a thunderclap. "Quiet!"

His shout jolted everyone present, even taking Sergeant Reynolds by surprise.

"We'll be interviewing all of you and taking statements." Acton's gaze swept across the room. "You can make your accusations, and the reasons for them, then." Acton's eyes landed on Gerry and Nellie. "We need an incident room, and I want it here in the house. Can you show my men a suitable space, please?"

Gerry accepted the request with a nod, and a puff on his pipe. He rose to his feet.

"Then we'll get started." As Acton moved to leave the room,

he issued final orders. "The rest of you, don't move from here until you're called to make a statement. And don't discuss the scene among yourselves. I want to hear what you know and witnessed, not what others have told you. Once I've spoken to you, you may go home, but you must remain available."

Well, he does like being the boss. And that's a good thing. We don't want someone who'll just let things take their course.

Acton exited the room, leaving a constable behind to enforce his directives.

His active pursuit for evidence might stimulate the locals to answer our questions, simply because they'll already be gossiping about what the police said, asked, or insinuated.

WITH THE STATEMENTS COLLECTED, the detectives were in conference in their makeshift incident room guarded by a vigilant constable stationed outside. The Marmalades, the girls, and Lady Mary congregated in the drawing room for coffee after an eerily quiet supper. The events of the day, the probing questions, and the weight of their statements lingered in the room, casting a shadow over the group.

Amid the hushed quiet, Barkley pitter-pattered down the hall and sauntered into the room also. His ears perked up, and his tail wagged energetically. The sudden appearance of the corgi broke the solemnity of the scene, if only momentarily.

"I told them what I saw and suggested they talk to you about the strange events leading up to today. I expect they did that." Mary paused to observe their expressions, gauging their reactions. "I hope that didn't cause either of you discomfort."

"Oh, I'm used to talking about this now," Nellie said with resignation, confirming the unusual occurrences had become a topic of discussion in their own right. "Margie shared her suspicions with everyone she has met, and I've been quelling the suggestion of certain doom ever since."

"But, Mum, for Mr. Beacham it *was* 'doom,' wasn't it."

Nellie paused, nonplussed, as though she'd only just considered the thought. "Well, I'm sure his death had nothing to do with the dead cat and dog," she said at last.

"I'm not," Mary said. "If someone was testing a dose to deliver—a cat, a dog, and then a man—it would be a logical progression."

"Really, Mary," Nellie said. "That's grotesque."

"Perhaps. Did the police ask anyone any surprising questions?" Mary asked.

"Not surprising," Nellie said. "Not after Fran's and Victor's outbursts. Really, those two should learn to govern their emotions better."

"I think Fran may have been upset at her husband's death, Mum," Margie said.

"I don't see why," her mother replied. "Everyone believes he's been carrying on with half the women in the village, and Rose in particular. You'd think she'd be pleased to be rid of him."

"But Nellie, dear," Mary said. "Just because someone no longer loves you doesn't mean you stop loving them. The world is full of such love triangles, as we must both remember from our younger days."

Nellie laughed. "Mary, we remember friends having wild affairs, but they were young people. Cyril, Rose and Fran weren't in the grip of youthful passion."

"Maybe they wanted one last fling. They do say when love hits older people, it hits them hard. Perhaps that's what happened here."

"You suspect Fran poisoned Cyril?" Nellie asked.

"Well, I'm not saying she did. Only that we can't rule it out," Mary replied.

Glaring at her mother, Margie announced defiantly, "I told the police Mr. Beacham was a man of loose morals who, I'd heard, was having affairs with many women in the village and probably elsewhere too."

"Margie!" her mother cried. "That's just gossip. We can't know that for certain."

Scowling, Margie quipped back, "You, I suppose, told them he was a saint."

Nellie colored. "I said he was a man who loved life and lived it to the fullest. He showed great energy and drive in everything he did."

Margie hooted with laughter. "That's what *I* said, only I was more honest."

Mary could see this exchange was about to become a mother-and-daughter row of the most exhausting kind. "As you say, Margie, you both described Mr. Beacham's character but from differing viewpoints. I'm sure the police will see that."

"They did," Winnie replied. "They asked me if he'd ever made a pass at me."

Dotty bobbed her head, her hair combed out extra frizzy today. "Me too."

"And your answers were?" Nellie asked.

"That we were only visitors and hadn't been here long enough for anything of that sort to happen," Winnie replied.

"But can we be clear? It didn't, did it?" Mary asked.

Winnie and Dotty glanced at each other before Dotty said, "No, it didn't. He's fond of married women, or so we've heard."

"Really, girls," Nellie said. "This isn't a fit subject for conversation."

"Mother!" Margie retorted. "We're not children. Everyone in

the village knew what Mr. Beacham was like. Everyone talked about it."

Nellie waved her hand. "Well, they shouldn't."

"But, Nellie," Mary replied, "the police can't ignore such a possible motive."

"The police will put the worst interpretation on anything they hear, and we shouldn't give them the ammunition to do that."

I hope the girls, particularly Margie, aren't drawing the same conclusions about Nellie's role in Cyril's life as I am from this discussion.

"There's also talk of wife-swapping," Dotty said nonchalantly, oblivious to the tension in the room.

Mary frowned. *There seems to be a lot more at stake than just the death of a neighbor, so where do we go from here? Maybe Margie is right, and it's the precarious personal side of Cyril that got him killed and not the business side. I do hope not. I'm too old to be untangling that 'love triangle drama' again.*

6

LET THE REAL GAMES BEGIN

"You see!" Nellie cried. "Wife-swapping in Upper Wainbury?! That's absurd."

Dotty wasn't fazed by Nellie's outburst. "It's just what I heard." She shrugged, her eyes cast down to the floor as she fiddled with the hem of her skirt.

"You shouldn't repeat gossip," Nellie snapped, her nostrils flaring.

"Gossip is sometimes the truth of what everyone knows but society can't or won't admit to," Mary said. "Everyone 'knows,' but we pretend it isn't there."

"Nonsense!" Nellie shrilled, and paced the room. "It's just malicious tittle-tattle, and repeating it should be a crime."

"If that's all it is, the police will sort it out," Margie said. "But, as Lady Mary said, someone could've been so badly hurt by it they murdered Mr. Beacham."

"It wasn't you, was it?" Winnie asked Margie, laughing.

Margie chuckled. "No, it wasn't me who murdered him."

"Okay, my chosen pupils, let's get clear of the gossip, truth or not. I need you all to be as open minded as you can be."

The girls assured her they were ready to investigate without any distracting baggage. "Where do we start, Lady Mary?" Margie questioned.

"This is in the hands of the police, Margie," her mother said firmly as she shot a pointed look at the girls. "It's best we leave it to them."

"Your mother is right," Mary added. "I know you'll be disappointed with what I'm saying, but now the police are involved, we should step back."

The three girls stared at her, eager gazes replaced by shocked expressions. Mary stared back with a blank look, hoping they would understand she had a strategy in mind she didn't want Nellie, or Gerry, knowing about.

Silence reigned for a moment, then Winnie agreed, keeping her eyes fixed on Mary's. "You're right. Our chance to investigate was before the murder."

The other two turned to Winnie, their mouths hanging open, and then Margie stormed out of the room. Nellie and Mary exchanged glances, and Nellie shrugged off her daughter's rudeness.

"I'll go after her," Mary said. "She won't like it, but she can take it out on me, not you, Nellie."

Outside, Mary found Margie stalking back and forth like a caged lion, muttering furiously.

When she saw Mary, Margie said, "I'm investigating. You can do as you please."

"I always do as I please." Mary chuckled. "I am a duchess."

Margie laughed in spite of herself and then pleaded with Mary. "We have to investigate, Lady Mary. You must see that."

"Of course we must," Mary replied, hugging Margie to her bosom. "But your mama and papa care about you, and they'll get in the way if they know that's what we're doing."

"I'm eighteen, for heaven's sake," Margie cried.

"You'll always be their child. You have to understand that,

and that sometimes you'll have to do things without their knowledge or approval. It's part of being an adult. Being your own person."

"You said we must investigate, so where do we start?"

"Can you round the girls up, secretly, of course, and we'll meet outside by the sycamore just before it gets dark?"

Margie nodded.

"Wonderful. Now let's return to the drawing room in harmony once again."

Nellie watched the two closely as they returned to their seats, but after a few moments, her back relaxed, and she sat with a satisfied expression.

Mary judged the moment right. "Nellie, you were going to show me your new rock garden. Perhaps we could do that before the light goes?"

"I was, wasn't I? With everything that's happened, I quite forgot. If you're finished with your coffee, we can do it now."

Mary followed Nellie out, pleased to see the girls staying back.

As they exited the French windows and walked along the terrace, Nellie said, "Since we had to give up on a full-time gardener, I've become interested. At first, I was angry about it. It wasn't how I imagined my older years, but now I love it. I see myself pruning roses until I'm ninety."

Mary laughed. "That's quite a change from the Nellie I remember."

"Aging is a great dream killer. We used to have such fun, didn't we?" She stared off at a distant memory.

"Mm-hmm." Mary deemed this a good time to ask. "You were adamant earlier that wife-swapping wasn't happening here. Was that just for the sake of the girls?"

"A bit, yes, but I wasn't lying. It isn't wife-swapping, exactly, but people do have affairs, sometimes just trysts. It's best the girls don't know about things like that until they have enough experience to understand life. And that it can be long and empty when you don't have things to fill it with."

"That's what all our parties were about," Mary agreed. "We just had nothing to fill our lives. I came to see that some years ago."

"Agreed. In a way, the war sobered us. And afterward, well, now we have work and activities to fill some of our time, like my gardening."

"But there are still free hours," Mary added.

"Exactly," Nellie replied as they arrived at a pile of rocks with plants interspersed, sloping up to an old stone wall. "What do you think?"

"Beautiful."

"It's at its best in the spring, but I've chosen the flowers to show well in each season."

"And it looks like you have," Mary said. "Who's having trysts with whom, Nellie?"

Nellie started at the blunt change of direction. "Oh, Cyril, of course. You wouldn't believe how attractive he was to women. Looking at him, and listening to him, you'd think we'd be repulsed, but there's no accounting for attraction, is there?"

"The police will want to know." Mary replied.

"They can get the dirt they need from others. I won't help them."

"I'm not the police, and I won't share with them what you told me, but I have some ideas about this murder, and this information will help point me in the right direction."

"You'll keep Margie out of this?"

"Margie is determined to investigate. It would be better if I guided and watched over her."

Nellie pondered this. "She's such a worry. Always doing the

opposite of what she's asked to do. We aren't asking for obedience, just sensible behavior."

"It's called teenage rebellion, and it's all the rage now, I hear." Mary chuckled.

Nellie sighed. "It's all so wearisome. Just when you think you're finished with their childish tantrums, it starts all over again."

Mary laughed. "We were pretty wild too, but they didn't have a label for it back then."

"It was the first war for us," Nellie said. "The boys were so glad to be out of it or happy they would never be in it. We just wanted to have fun."

Mary nodded. "But it left us with the idea that, once the heir and the spare were born, we could all have alternate partners, which is why I don't believe it was only Cyril here in Upper Wainbury."

Nellie shuffled uncomfortably. "Cyril liked women, it's true, but Fran tried to punish him by having her own affairs with the husbands of Cyril's lovers."

"But no one else?" Mary asked.

Nellie nodded.

"I find that unlikely."

"We're a small village," Nellie replied. "There isn't a large number of people willing to become adulterers." She paused. "If you question them, people might suggest I'm having an affair with Victor Illingsworth. It isn't true. He and I are on the Parish Council, and we have similar views on subjects, so we often get together to plan our joint strategies."

"Does Gerry think you're having an affair?"

"Of course not," Nellie balked. "But he and Rose also have interests in common, so you can see how some of the rumors behind the wife-swapping story come from our relationship with the Illingsworths."

"I see. Between you all, you've made a tangled web for the police to unwind. It would be better to tell them straight out."

"I'll talk to Victor, and if he agrees, we'll tell them. I'll leave the others to tell their own stories."

"Upper Wainbury has become quite a little Peyton Place," Mary said, through a stifled laugh, as they turned back toward the house.

"Don't be silly, Mary. It's nothing like that."

"There are the girls, up on the terrace." Mary gestured as Margie, Dotty, and Winnie were coming to join them.

"Nothing of this to them, Mary, please," Nellie begged. "I'll never forgive you if Margie believes I'm having an affair with Victor Illingsworth."

"She may already suspect that, Nellie, which may be why you're having trouble with her."

"We came to find out what happened to you both," Winnie said, breaking into the conversation. "We thought you might have met your demise too."

"Really, Winnie." Nellie cringed. "This isn't a joke."

"We know," Margie replied seriously. "Which is why we came outside."

"Well, now you're here." Mary's lips curved into a friendly smile. She gestured subtly with her head, indicating the expanse of the grounds beyond. "Join us for a stroll."

"Gerry will be all alone in the house, and he'll brood," Nellie mused. "I'll go and talk to him about our discussion."

"Good idea." Mary glanced toward the assembled girls, a silent signal passing between them, and added, "The girls and I will walk." Nellie resolutely turned toward the house and rushed off.

With that Mary led the way as they strolled across the grounds toward the tennis court. Spotting Nellie's silhouette disappearing indoors, Mary's gaze turned serious. "Now, there are things we need to discuss."

"We've been thinking," Margie started, her words measured. "We—well, I, mainly—are best placed to uncover if the wife-swapping motive has anything to it."

"I agree," Mary affirmed. "Ponsonby can start on Beacham's art gallery and business, and Cook can ferret out other undercurrents from the servants of all the local houses."

"What about you?" Dotty asked Mary.

"You remember in our last case we had a nice young artist help with a scarab brooch?"

Dotty traced her finger along the ivy-covered trellis as the sunlight diminished. They strode along the path while Mary laid out her idea. "I had the notion I would visit him and learn what the art world thinks of Mr. Beacham, as my starting point."

"What about the antiques side of Beacham's business?" Winnie asked. "We can't forget that."

"Nor will we. When we were refurnishing Snodsbury and Culpeper House, we used a respectable London company, and I'll inquire with them for the information."

"There's something else." Margie frowned. "It didn't come out today in any of the conversations, but Fran Beacham told Mum some time ago that they were getting anonymous letters threatening Cyril."

"Nellie never mentioned that," Mary muttered.

"She hasn't mentioned it since that day," Margie said. "So I don't know if it's true or not. Or why she would omit it now."

"Does the village have one of those old-fashioned nosy postmistresses?" Mary inquired.

Margie giggled. "Mrs. Higgins is exactly that. She listens in on conversations as well. Having the mail and the telephone in one place is a source of great delight to the Higginses of the world."

"Then we need to get Mrs. Higgins talking," Mary suggested. "How best to do that?"

"Gin!" Margie perked up, laughing. "Oh, and a visit from a real live duchess, of course. She's hot about the royal family and aristocracy."

"Then that'll be my task tomorrow," Mary said, her gaze fixed ahead on the tennis court. "Any other thoughts?" She peered at each of her sleuths.

Silence settled among them, save for a soft rustling of leaves and the distant trill of a bird. Suddenly, Barkley burst out of the bushes and padded over to them, his tail wagging as he sniffed at the ground curiously.

"We start tomorrow," Mary declared. She paused, eyeing Barkley. "But no one must know what we're up to."

His nose twitched, and he let out a low, uncertain growl and in the dark of the evening a strange foreboding settled over Mary.

7

DEUCES AND DECEPTIONS

Inspector Acton and his team arrived back at the house early the following morning. *At least he's an active detective,* Mary reflected, but it was a problem for her. She'd hoped to escape to the village unseen. *Fortunately, Ponsonby had taken the early morning milk train to London and was outside the reach of officious officers.*

"We have a warrant to search this house and gardens." Acton handed the paperwork to Gerry.

"What on earth for?" Gerry demanded, staring at the warrant in disbelief.

Acton passed Gerry without replying, barging into the hall.

Reynolds stepped aside. "The victim died of nicotine poisoning."

"He only smoked the occasional cigar," Gerry retorted. "He didn't consume, he savored them."

"More likely the poison is in the house or garden shed, intended for killing garden pests. That stuff can contain nicotine," Reynolds said, as he too pushed past Gerry rooted in the doorway.

"But he wouldn't drink weed killer or any household

poison," Gerry complained as he followed Reynolds. "They all smell and taste too horrible."

"The blackstrap rum in his flask could have been laced with it," Reynolds speculated. "He might have taken a swig without noticing the taste."

"Nonsense," Gerry replied. "Cyril drank rum all the time. He'd have noticed."

"That may be, sir," Reynolds said amiably. "But we have to search for the source of the poison, and where the victim died is as good a place as any to start."

The discussion continued into the morning room, which gave Mary the chance to set out on her own investigation. She walked up to her chamber, donned a hat and coat, and then left the house by the servants' door. The police were diligently searching the grounds, but no one was guarding the gate as Mary walked down the drive and into the lane.

A quick walk to the village and the post office was easy to find. It was the most prominent shop on the main street with its postal emblem hanging above the entrance. A sign above the door listed Mrs. G. Higgins as Postmistress. The door squealed as Mary opened it, and the bell overhead jingled as she entered. Instead of finding Mrs. Higgins, Mary found a mousy man behind the counter.

"Good morning," Mary greeted him. "A beautiful morning for a stroll."

"Beautiful," the man mumbled in reply.

"I need stamps," Mary asked. "But I shall browse for a moment if you don't mind."

"Not at all, madam. Is there something in particular?"

Like all such places, the village post office carried a selection of small items likely to be needed by the local people: dried and canned food, stationery, dress and knitting patterns, string and glue, small toys, and copious amounts of sugared treats for children and those with a sweet tooth.

"I hardly know. I'm staying with the Marmalades and have been invited to a house with a small boy today. I must take a present—a toy or a book, maybe, but I'm not sure."

The man's expression changed from dour to bewildered, and he glanced at a side door. "My wife will be better able to help." He darted away.

She smiled at subdued whispering through the side door: "It's that duchess." A minute later, a bustling woman with twice the life of her partner opened the door and walked around the counter. She approached Mary. "You must be the Duchess of Snodsbury. We heard you were visiting."

Mary smiled. "I am. I'm visiting with the Marmalades as you may know." The woman nodded and Mary continued, "Nellie Marmalade and I were at school together a lifetime ago and long before I became a duchess."

"It's an honor to welcome Your Grace to our post office," Mrs. Higgins said. "My husband told me you're looking for a toy for a boy. We have some gifts here in the corner that might suit you. Not a large selection, I'm afraid. We only have sufficient for the village's last-minute needs."

"Thank you." Mary followed her to the toys on shelves out of the reach of children. "Maybe that car would be nice. Does it make sounds?"

Mrs. Higgins took down the box and showed Mary the illustration—a wind-up police car with a key, and a bell that clanged as the car ran along.

"Yes, I think a small boy would like that, especially if the bell ringing drives his parents mad." Mary chortled.

"Shall I wrap it for you?" Mrs. Higgins hurried away before Mary answered.

"I expect you'll know everyone who resides in the village," Mary called after her, "being the postmistress."

Mrs. Higgins returned with a sheet of paper and a length of twine. "Oh, yes, Your Grace. Everyone comes in here sometime during the week, and Joe delivers the mail, so we're the center of village life." She beamed, her eyes bright, her plump cheeks pink and her graying hair pulled back into a neat bun.

Mary peered around the shop and lowered her voice, though there was no one else in the room. "I expect you heard what happened?"

With another nod, Mrs. Higgins whispered, "Everybody has heard. We've never had anything like this in the village. At least as long as I've lived here, and that's nigh on forty years."

"As the center of village life, do you have any thoughts on who might have wanted Mr. Beacham dead? We at the house can't account for it at all."

"It's funny you should ask, but Mr. Beacham was a shifty sort of bloke. And lately he'd been getting letters." She nodded meaningfully.

"More letters than usual, you mean?"

Mrs. Higgins shook her head. "Different letters. When the first arrived, he came in here and accused my husband and me of sending it. We had a hard time convincing him we'd never sent him any such letter. And why would we? He only lives a hop, skip, and a jump from here, and his wife is here often enough for the conveyance of any messages."

"That must have been very upsetting for you."

"It was. Quite shook me up, I can tell you. Mr. Beacham was a very passionate man when angry."

"He didn't say what the letters were about?"

"No, but I watched out for them and saw them arrive. He had plenty of business correspondence daily, but once in a while, about every month or so for the past six months, he'd get a letter in a plain envelope, the kind you can buy anywhere, handwritten, by a man, I'd say. Postmarked in London. When the second letter arrived, I said to my husband, Joe, 'Here's another one of them letters; we'll have Beacham here post haste.' But the strange thing was, he never came after that first one."

"When he was complaining," Mary asked, "did he give a hint at why he didn't like the letter?"

The woman snorted. "He said it was libelous and if I wrote it, I would hear from his lawyer."

"But not why it was libelous?"

Mrs. Higgins twisted her face in deep thought. "He said it was a lie. None of his artwork was looted, which was odd. We normally say 'stolen,' don't we?"

"Normally, we do," Mary agreed thoughtfully. "There's nothing else you can remember?"

She shook her head. "He ranted for a long time, but it was just repeating what he'd already said, that if I'd written this letter I could expect to hear from his lawyer and I wouldn't get a penny out of him."

Blackmail?

"But you were able to satisfy him it wasn't you?"

"I didn't think so. That's why I thought when I saw the second letter, he'd come back. When the others arrived and he still didn't come back, and his lawyer hadn't been in touch, I assumed I had persuaded him it wasn't me. And it couldn't have been me. I've never been to London, and I had no idea he was suspected of stealing antiques." She paused. "Or was it artwork? I can't remember."

The bell chimed as a customer entered. "Well," Mary said. "I'll take the toy car and a book of stamps, thank you, Mrs. Higgins."

"Morning," Mary greeted the new customer as the postmistress finished the wrapping and rang the purchases into the till.

Mary was gathering her purchases as Mrs. Higgins also welcomed the newcomer and then cried to Mary, "Oh, I've just remembered something!"

Mary spun to hear what it was.

"Now it's gone again," Mrs. Higgins said. "I'm sorry, it was right on the tip of my tongue."

She's provided good information about the mysterious letters, maybe she'll have a bit more. "I have another errand to run," Mary said. "Perhaps I can call in on my way back. It may come back to you."

"Likely it will, Your Grace. I'll be forgetting my own head one day, I'm getting so forgetful."

Mary left the post office and walked along the quaint street, lost in thought as she weighed the potential value of the newfound information against the price it might exact from her —needing to purchase something at every inquiry. *The letters could likely have been business related, or sexual. Seems a stronger motive to be business than middle-aged affairs in the countryside. Speaking to my London connections may well provide the break-through I need.*

While her mind whirled on, Mary was window-shopping at the butcher's and almost missed the customer leaving the post office. *What additional information does Mrs. Higgins have to sell?*

Mary hurried back before any other customers arrived.

"Your Grace," the postmistress said as Mary reentered the shop. "That was quick."

"Has your memory recovered?" Mary felt she didn't need to explain.

Mrs. Higgins looked grave, sorrowful even. "It's like this, Your Grace. I'm so worried these days with bills and the slump in business and everything else going on, things get driven out of my mind."

"I can understand that," Mary said sympathetically. "I've also struggled these years since the war. Is there a pressing problem you have right now I might help with?"

"That is kind of you, Your Grace, but I couldn't ask anything for myself. We try to help our son along in his new business, and, well, it would be an investment in the community, if you could help."

"Would five pounds help?" Mary asked bluntly, expecting this could go on all day if she allowed it.

"It would help more than you could imagine." Mrs. Higgins beamed.

Mary took the note from her purse and handed it over. Mrs. Higgins folded it into her bra and buttoned up her blouse.

"What I remembered," she said, leaning over the counter with a serious expression, "was that your friend, Mr. Marmalade, received those letters as well. Or at least they appeared the same to me. Only two of them, mind you, not as many as Mr. Beacham."

Mary thanked her and left the shop. *What had Gerry to do with all this? Was there a connection between Gerry and Beacham? One was a London art dealer, the other a county justice of the peace, so it wasn't a business connection. What could Gerry and Cyril have in common that a blackmailer thought worth the attempt? And had either of the two men paid the blackmailer?*

LATER THAT EVENING, before Mary met up with her young assistants to learn what they'd discovered on the village gossip circuit, Ponsonby arrived back from London. Mary still pondered her next move. *If I alert the police, they may be able to see Gerry's and Cyril's bank accounts. They must already have requested access to Cyril's at least. If I ask Inspector Acton, would he tell me of any unusual payments?*

Mary sent word for Cook and Ponsonby to meet in her room the moment he'd had time to recover from the journey.

"Tell us what you have uncovered," Mary prompted. "Particularly, what you learned at Beacham's art gallery."

"I don't yet know who killed Mr. Beacham, but we should definitely frame his business partner for it," Ponsonby replied.

Mary chuckled. "Was it as bad as that?"

"Yes, my lady. Auric Winkler is a truly odious man. I didn't let him know who I was—as far as he knew, I was just a customer who'd learned of Mr. Beacham's death. Yet the man oozed artificial sorrow. He slyly implied his now-dead partner was someone he'd distanced himself from. He was so concerned to assure me, a random customer, that whatever wrongdoing would come to light in the investigation, none should reflect on him nor the gallery."

"He must be very shaken to be so defensive."

"Indeed, my lady," Ponsonby said. "A creature without courage or honor. A modern day Uriah Heep, if ever I saw one."

"And your opinion of the gallery?"

"I've no doubt the gallery and its now-owner are neck-deep in whatever it was Beacham was doing."

"So there's a strong motive there. Could he have come here on Saturday or Sunday and laced Beacham's drink?" Mary asked.

"I examined the train timetables," Ponsonby said, "and, yes, in theory it could be done. I also quietly reconnoitered the gallery for a motorcycle but didn't find one. He may have one at his home, but we have no way of knowing. Unfortunately, thanks to the train timetables for my own return, I couldn't wait to follow him after the gallery closed. The gallery keeps evening hours along with their daytime ones."

Cook arrived with a tray of tea, and Mary confirmed to Ponsonby, "We'll check for a motorcycle when we're in London to meet the artist."

"To be honest, my lady, I can't imagine a man as paltry as Winkler ever riding a motorcycle."

Mary smiled and turned to Cook. "What did you learn among the different households?"

"Not much yet, Lady Mary. I'm still winning them over. I hope to know more very soon because one or two people, on learning I'm the famous Lady Mary's cook, clearly wanted to chat, but away from the others."

"Tomorrow, then." Mary clapped.

"Yes, milady." Cook poured three cups of tea and served Mary.

"You must give them the chance to meet you alone," Mary added, accepting the teacup. "For now—this evening, I mean—we must find a way to get the girls away from Nellie."

"I've heard Mr. Marmalade is at the golf course," Cook interjected. "Mrs. Marmalade will want those young ladies around to keep her amused."

Acknowledging the difficulty, Mary tipped her head. *The real problem, however, isn't getting the girls away from Nellie but getting Nellie away from me. Nellie wants to continuously catch up on everything she doesn't know about my life and in turn tell me everything about her own.*

MARY DISMISSED Ponsonby and Cook for the evening and made her way to the drawing room, where Nellie and the girls were comfortably chatting. And her fears were justified—it was only when Gerry returned from the golf course that Nellie left Mary's side and retired with him for the evening, giving Mary her chance to speak to her junior sleuths.

She found the girls too had been patiently waiting to be alone and pounced the moment the coast was clear, all speaking at once in their haste to tell Mary everything they'd learned.

She held up her hand. "One at a time, ladies, please."

Margie began, "Some of the stories are too unbelievable to be true."

"The stories surrounding our principal character are of the most interest," Mary replied. "Though there's a possibility of someone we know nothing about being the culprit, so we shouldn't discount anyone at this stage."

Margie added, "It's clear Mr. Beacham was a busy man in all the years he's lived here in the village."

"We can discount the vicar's wife," Winnie noted. "She's ninety if she's a day. I'm certain she hasn't anything to do with the case."

The others giggled. "And old Miss Goforth," Dotty added. Her attention darted to the windows. "She'll die of shock if she hears she's being gossiped about this way. She was away visiting her daughter."

"Well, for now we can put them to one side. Now what of the other villagers?"

"It was confirmed by several people his affair with Mrs. Illingsworth had been going on for some time," Winnie revealed. "Though it takes pride of place in the gossip, no one offered the name of who came before her."

"Someone could've waited a while to kill him so his death wouldn't be connected to an earlier affair," Dotty said. "But they'd have to be very patient—he and Rose had been seeing each other for more than a year by now."

Mary's thoughts churned. *A year might carry different weight for various individuals.* She considered the complexities of human emotions and the entanglements of mature relationships. *The girls are right, we can't completely rule out revenge by a jilted lover, or a jilted lover's husband.*

Margie, who'd been quiet while the others theorized, spoke up. "I don't think his death is related to these affairs. The stories we heard told of secretive affairs among ordinary private people. Nothing like a grand passion that might lead to murder."

Dotty shared her agreement with two thumbs-up, and Winnie added, "I agree. We have to keep it in mind as a motive, but if it's related to these affairs, it's likely not from passion."

"If it isn't passion, as you say," Mary responded, "could it be something like greed? Suppose one of Beacham's lovers was rich and her husband believed she wanted to leave him and take his money with her."

The girls exchanged glances. "We didn't think of that," Margie said at last. "There could be other motives still. We must follow up on that tomorrow."

"And the motorcycle?" Mary asked. "Did anyone else hear it?"

"Mrs. Wetherspoon lives on the road leading to the new road," Winnie said. "She remembers a motorcycle roaring out of the village one night, but she's not sure what night it was."

"Very well. This has been a good start. Now I'll tell you what Ponsonby, Cook and I learned."

She briefly outlined the information, leaving out the part about Margie's father getting letters like Beacham's, and paused for the team's thoughts.

"We need to know if that partner has a motorcycle," Winnie said. "Or access to one. If Ponsonby thinks he's bad, I'm convinced."

"Ponsonby and I will return to London tomorrow to investigate from there. Cook will continue inveigling her way into the local servants' confidence to give us even more about the villagers. You three need to keep working on the neighbors for possible motives. Don't just investigate the motive I mentioned—find out if anyone can suggest another. After all, there are *seven* deadly sins, and we've only touched on two of them."

"Mine is not a churchy family," Winnie commented. "What exactly are the seven deadly sins?"

Mary smiled. "I remember from school days, so you who've just left school should. They're pride, greed, lust, envy, gluttony, wrath, and sloth. We've decided lust isn't likely, based on the characters. There's still the possibility of pride and wrath from an irate husband, though unlikely, and I've suggested greed may be possible. I can't figure out how envy, gluttony or sloth might be a motive, but we can't rule them out."

"And that's what we must discover," Dotty said. "Other motives that can come from illicit affairs among people who have lots to lose."

Winnie straightened. "But have they? Despite the lurid stories we heard, none of these have any heat in them. Nor do these people behave like they would lose their heads, or their positions, or possessions, over any of this."

"Dig deeper," Mary said. "If nothing has come to light by this time tomorrow, when I'm back from London, we'll look elsewhere, locally. Maybe Cook will dig up something new from the servants."

8

BACKHAND WHISPERS

The next morning, Mary was up with the servants. Ponsonby and Cook, however, were ready before her, and breakfast was laid out when she descended from her room. Barkley too was fed earlier than usual and, after finishing in a few swift gulps, came and sat by Mary as she ate.

Mary stroked his ears. "I'm sorry, Barkley, but you have to stay with the girls today. My visit to London will be all work and no play."

Barkley's expression said he understood but didn't approve. *Could he remember London and the knife-wielding man in the park? Does he worry an old man like Ponsonby won't be adequate protection?*

"It's no good looking at me like that," Mary said, divining his thoughts. "You must stay and help the girls in their investigations."

At this, Barkley rose to his feet with great dignity and left the room.

Once her meal was concluded, Ponsonby drove Lady Mary to the station, where they both boarded the morning train to Bristol. At Bristol, they changed to the London train, and by late morning, they were back at Culpeper House, Mary's London home.

"While I'm phoning or meeting our artist friend," Mary told Ponsonby, "you go along to Companies House and investigate that gallery and business. There must be something. Also, phone the furniture people we used. They'll be aware of someone who has information. We'll visit their offices together after lunch."

Mary phoned the artist's studio and received no answer. She called Eleanor Fortescue at the Palace and was pleasantly surprised to connect at once. She explained she needed to talk to the jeweler who'd made the false scarab when they were investigating the death of Lady Hilary Sinclair.

"He's an artist," Eleanor said. "He likely won't be out of bed till noon."

"But he still works out of the same studio?"

"Oh, yes, Lady Mary. I would just let him get up and get dressed before you knock on his door."

Amusement warmed Mary's voice. "Thank you. We'll speak again soon. Oh, before I disconnect, remind me of his name."

"It's Rupert, and be cautious, Lady Mary, he'd become very strange when I last saw him. Sadly, I think he's partaking in hallucinogens."

"I'm sorry to hear that," Mary said, before ending the call and then phoning for a taxi. *Maybe I shouldn't go alone—but I will anyway. What harm can he be?*

The studio was in darkness when Mary hammered on the metal door. It took some time before a disheveled face appeared at the window. His expression changed from a perturbed scowl to one of remembrance, and he flashed Mary a broad grin. The door opened, and with a comical bow and sweep of his hand, he gestured for her to enter, which she did.

Mary at once saw why Eleanor had advised her to wait until he was dressed. In the gloom, the robe he was wearing looked filthy. *It's just paint,* she told herself. His scrawny legs and feet poked out of the skirt, and his equally skinny arms from the sleeves. *Has he not eaten in weeks?* She grimaced at the unhealthy grayness of his face.

"What can I do for Your Ladyship at this ridiculous time of day?"

Clearly polite conversation wasn't required, so Mary simply asked. "What can you tell me about Beacham and Winkler's, the art gallery?"

"Not a lot," the man replied. "They don't sell my work." He gestured for her to follow him.

"Your choice or theirs?" she asked as she dodged strange objects littered around the hall.

"Both, I imagine." Rupert walked toward a table where cigarettes and a lighter lay. He placed a cigarette between his lips and, with shaking hands, lit it.

"Why yours, then?" she asked, resigned to have to tolerate the smoke.

"They're crooks," he replied, "which would be all right if they would be decent to the artists whose work they sell, but they're not."

A big puff of smoke passed her nose, and she held her breath while asking, "Why do you say they're crooks?"

He shrugged. "Everyone says so." He flicked his ashes onto the floor and walked into the room to his right, switching on the light as she entered behind him.

She gazed around at the mess. "But you don't have actual evidence of wrongdoing?"

"What's all this about?" He turned, peering at her suspiciously with the cigarette dangling from his lips.

"Beacham died at my friend Nellie's place on the weekend,

and I want to know why. I speculate his business or dealings might be the motive."

He shuffled a stack of papers from an old tattered couch and offered her a seat.

She politely shook her head, declining the invitation. "I'll stand. I won't take up much of your time."

"Suit yourself. It could be. Motive..." He paused, and closed his eyes as if considering. When his eyes popped open, he confessed, "Look, you didn't hear this from me, but when I was at their gallery, trying to sell some pieces, I saw something that shouldn't have been there. I knew of the piece, and I was aware of where the real one was."

She narrowed her eyes. "You didn't challenge them on it?"

His eyebrows shot up. "Are you mad?" he retorted, his tone a blend of mock exasperation and self-preservation. "I was hoping to make a sale, not end up in the Thames with a concrete block around my feet."

A dry chuckle escaped her lips, her skepticism giving way to amusement. "Are you suggesting they're gangsters?"

That's hard to believe, what with Ponsonby's description of Winkler.

He shook his head—disbelief and wariness clouding his expression. "But I saw a real one in their office while I was there. A real live mobster. If they're working with people like that, I don't want to know. I left before I saw any more."

Mary's brow furrowed, her curiosity piqued. "How do you recognize a gangster?"

"If you live in the city, you know who they are." He slugged on his cigarette and blew another blast of smoke past her face.

Mary back up slightly. "Then the police must too."

"I'm sure they know," he said with the cigarette hanging from his lips before securing it between his teeth. "But proving wrongdoing is the problem. No one would testify against these gangs."

"If Beacham and Winkler's gallery is operated by criminals or they're in league with them, then they must be selling stolen or forged goods, wouldn't you say?" Mary asked as he leaned against the doorjamb. "You witnessed something forged—did you see anything else?"

He shook his head and ashes floated in the air. "I told you, I realized quickly my health depended on me not seeing anything else in that gallery, and I got out."

"There's nothing you can add, or any leads you would suggest I follow?"

"No. If you know what's good for you, you'll stay out of it. Now please leave. If you want a nice jewel created, come again, but otherwise, we have nothing to discuss."

Mary left the studio and entered the waiting taxi. "Culpeper House, please," she told the driver, and stretched out in the backseat to consider what she'd learned as the cab wended its way through the busy streets.

Beacham's business dealings were as crooked as they were rumored to be. Was he killed by the criminals, and that's what Winkler fears? That he'll be next? Was Gerry somehow implicated in these crooked sales, and that's why he received those two anonymous letters? If so, the sender must be someone who knew of the gallery's criminal acts. That means Winkler, or did they have other staff?

She was still running through these questions, without being any closer to answering them, when the cab pulled up at Culpeper House.

Ponsonby returned minutes later, and they quickly compared their morning's meager information. He had also arranged a meeting for her with the director of the company who'd provided the furniture for Culpeper House's renovation.

They had time for a brief lunch, then they were back on the trail. While Ponsonby waited with her cab, Mary was escorted to the managing director's office by a smartly dressed, silent secretary. The secretary announced Mary and left the two, closing the door behind her.

"We know *of* Beacham and Winkler, Lady Mary," the managing director told her coldly when she posed her question. "We would never do business with them."

"They're known to be dishonest, then?"

"They were once a reputable company, but now . . ." He left the sentence unfinished.

"When did the change happen?" Mary asked. "Was it recent?"

"It's hard to be precise in these matters. I'd say it was when Beacham stepped back from the day-to-day running of the gallery. Whether he's aware of what is going on or not, I couldn't say."

"I'm afraid he's dead. He died at a friend's house on the weekend. I was there, and something about what happened has set the police investigating, and it made me suspicious, also."

"One is always sorry to hear of sudden deaths of people one knows," the managing director said.

"What kind of things made your company stop dealing with them?"

"The first time, we were supplied with a sculpture that was sold as an original. It was not an original," he replied. "On that occasion, they appeared as shocked as we were, but it happened a second time. A painting this time. They're still on our list of possible suppliers, but between you and me, we will never do business with them again."

"You haven't heard of them being involved with mobsters or anything like that?"

He hesitated. "There have been rumors, but we'd already decided to sever our ties with them, so it's not our concern."

"I wondered if his death had something to do with Mr. Beacham's business," Mary said. "It's hard to imagine anyone in Upper Wainbury summoning the energy to kill a neighbor, to be honest."

He laughed. "I agree his business interests are more likely, but you know what they say about still waters—they run deep. Sleepy villages can harbor strong resentments over trivial matters. I speak from experience. We, my wife and I, have a cottage in the Cotswolds that we go to whenever we can, and you'd be astonished at the passions aroused over the smallest of incidents."

"The Miss Marple view of the world, I see." Mary smiled. "All the evils of the world to be found in everyday village life."

"My wife is a great fan of Miss Marple." He grinned. "I think she secretly hopes one day for a murder near our cottage so she can solve it."

"That's the position in which I find myself," Mary replied. "A visit to an old friend, a murder, and the county police looking in from the outside. As an insider, I feel I can help them a lot. They haven't yet expressed an opinion on wanting my help, but I'm hopeful, especially if I can give them good information they'd find difficult to gather themselves."

"Then here's something I heard years ago, but I have no idea if it's true." He lowered his voice and leaned closer. "Cyril Beacham was into illicit dealings in Germany at the end of the war. Stolen artwork and that kind of thing. I've no idea if it's true, and I never heard it again."

"Who told you? Was it someone in the trade?"

He shook his head. "It was years ago at a memorial service

for my son who was killed in France. Beacham was there—we were still doing business then, you see. An ex-officer from my son's regiment recognized him and asked me his name. When I told him, he told me what I've just relayed to you. Beacham was suspected of trading in stolen, looted artwork in the early days of our occupation of Berlin."

"You didn't question him about it?"

"No. Even the man I conversed with specifically said 'suspected' and not factual. But it was in my mind the moment we were sold that first dodgy item, and then I made up my mind when we had the second."

"He couldn't have been caught, if he was looting artwork," Mary mused, "or he never would be able to be working in the trade now."

"From what I've heard, there was an investigation, but it was so badly managed, Beacham came out smelling of roses. The chap who ran the investigation, Major Marmalade, was suspected of deliberately helping Beacham evade authorities."

Major Marmalade, hmm... An implication of Gerry's complicity in this crime. Could explain why they both received letters. Mary bobbed her head. "Thank you, I won't take any more of your time." She left his office, and he escorted her outside to the awaiting taxi. Her thoughts churning.

With Garry's involvement, the plot thickens, whether for the good or bad? Now I know what connects them, and it means the letters weren't about recent crooked dealings but possibly the distant past. Who would know more of that time?

Ponsonby assisted Mary into the cab, then joined her in the backseat.

She needed a moment to take stock of what she'd learned.

Ponsonby slid the glass partition between the driver and passengers firmly shut. "Well, my lady? Did you learn anything significant?"

"Indeed I did. We have a real motive and a credible suspect, unfortunately."

"Unfortunately?"

Mary explained her conversation and the possibility of Gerry's involvement.

"This is unfortunate indeed. Do you think young Miss Marmalade has any suspicions?"

"I hope not. But Nellie should. She must know."

They drove in silence for a few minutes as the driver negotiated a busy intersection, before Ponsonby noted, "It's unlikely a blackmailer would murder his victim. After all, that's where the money is."

"But a man who has social standing may murder someone who is a threat to him, even if he's also the blackmailer's victim."

Ponsonby volleyed back, "And the man's wife may be even more determined to remove a problem, if it threatens her *family*. Deadlier than a male, they do say."

"None of which makes this a happy lead to follow," Mary remarked, her frustration unhidden. "And we can only be a few hours ahead of the police by this point. I'm sure they'll know what we know very soon."

"We must be quick to exonerate our hosts," Ponsonby replied. He glanced at Mary. "If they're innocent."

"They've been surprisingly reticent with us about their involvement, if they are," Mary replied. "But before we leave London, I wish to visit this gallery I've heard so much about." She announced the address to the driver, and thirty minutes later, the taxi was parked across from the business.

"Wait here," Mary said, leaving the cab. "I won't be long."

When Mary returned, Ponsonby and the driver were deep in conversation.

"Well, he's an unpleasant man!" Mary huffed as she slipped

into the backseat of the taxi beside Ponsonby. "Did you by any chance examine the back of the building?"

Ponsonby smiled. "I did. I walked along the alley." He pointed as the taxi pulled away. "Sadly, again, there was no sign of a motorcycle. We need to find his home to confirm if he's the owner of the mysterious motorbike people heard that night."

"It's frustrating, but it could just be a coincidence."

"That's true, it could be, and no one mentioned hearing it on the night before Beacham's death, so it may be insignificant."

At Culpeper House, their conversation ended, temporarily, as Mary left to freshen up. There'd be plenty of time to talk during the journey back to Upper Wainbury.

As Mary refreshed her makeup in front of the bedroom mirror, she reviewed back over what she'd heard. Now she knew why Gerry had been so insistent Cyril's death was of natural causes; he didn't want to even think it was murder. Was she right about that, or was he the murderer and hoped to deflect the investigation? Surely not. He heard court cases all day, and if he was the killer, he must have known the police would find poison in Cyril's body. She hoped that meant he wasn't. She'd known Gerry almost as long as she'd known Nellie, and to find he was the murderer would be awful. Nellie would never forgive her—and nor would Margie. There was a lesson for her: never take on a case where family and friends are involved. She had few enough friends left now, and to lose them this way was unthinkable.

When Ponsonby informed her the cab had arrived to take them to the station, Mary was forced back into the real world.

"I hope Cook and our fellow sleuths have plenty to tell us when we get back to Upper Wainbury," Mary said. "I don't want to divulge everything told to me today, and having them tell us their successes will make that easier to achieve."

"Indeed, my lady," Ponsonby replied. "The knowledge we've received bodes badly for the Marmalade family, I fear."

Should I inform the police? I should, but what if it isn't true? Nellie and Gerry would never forgive me for ruining their lives over a baseless accusation. I'm fairly sure the police will find this out for themselves soon enough without me involving our self proclaimed band of sleuths—the Society of Six as we'd duly named it.

What if they don't? Do I point them in Gerry's direction? He's lived quietly in the country, a blameless life since the war, and that could end if he's arrested for something I said—even if it turns out not to be true.

I should stop investigating now. But if Gerry's innocent and the police learn what I've just learned, can I be sure he'll be cleared of all wrongdoing? Innocent people are sometimes found guilty. The only way I can prevent that is to go on investigating.

If the police haven't found this connection in the next two days, I'll tell them and ask for my part to be kept secret. Will Acton accept that? Here's hoping it doesn't happen.

9

GAME, SET, MYSTERY

As Mary and Ponsonby arrived at the Marmalades' manor, the trio of assistant sleuths emerged from the concealment of the bushes, waving animatedly to flag down the approaching vehicle. The car came to a halt, and before Ponsonby could step out to assist them, Margie, Dotty and Winnie had swiftly piled into the backseat beside Mary. Barkley was last to enter, and he walked over all their laps to sit in his rightful place with Mary. Barkley nestled himself comfortably, his tail wagging with contentment as he settled in.

Eyes shining with eagerness, Winnie leaned forward and blurted, "What do you think?"

Mary arched an eyebrow in bemusement. "About what?"

Winnie replied, "Today!"

"I don't follow?"

"The police have taken Mr. Illingsworth into custody," Winnie replied.

A chorus of voices followed. "Practically arrested him," Margie interjected.

"For questioning," Dotty chimed in.

A faint sigh escaped Mary's lips, a mix of understanding and resignation. "Oh dear. Well, I'm not too surprised. The police do like to be methodical."

Margie's curiosity remained unquenched, her eyes fixed on Mary's face. "What? You don't think he did it?"

"Ohhh, you know who did it?" Winnie cried.

Mary's response was calm and composed. "It's too early to know who did it," she said, repressing their excitement. "We don't have all the facts."

"Was Ponsonby right about the gallery owner?" Dotty asked as she played with Barkley's ears.

"We came back too early to follow Mr. Winkler home, so we don't yet know if he's the mystery motorcyclist," Mary explained. "That will have to wait. We did get more information about Beacham's business affairs, which I'll tell you about later. Now you tell me what you've learned today and what the police said about Mr. Illingsworth."

As they exited the car, Nellie came out to welcome Mary back. And Barkley bounded inside, chasing the smell of fresh-baked goodies.

"Did you learn anything useful, Mary?"

Is that a shade of anxiety in Nellie's voice? And does that mean she thinks I now know about Gerry's involvement in looting art treasure in Berlin in 1945?

"I did," Mary said. "But we can discuss it later. I need to freshen myself after the day."

"You smell like smoke and soot." Dotty wrinkled her nose.

Mary chuckled. *That's the least of it.* "I generally dislike modern improvements, but I really think the sooner steam trains are gone, the better. I feel like a chimney sweep must feel at the end of his working day."

Nellie laughed, linked arms with her friend, and they entered the house together. "Well," she said, releasing Mary's arm at the foot of the stairs. "I'll contain my curiosity for an hour longer. After dinner, we can chat. The girls are going to a dance."

"A dance?"

"It has been the Wainbury Agricultural Show since last week, and today is the final day. There's always a dance in the evening. The girls are pretending to be country folk tonight."

Mary and Nellie followed in the wake of the chatter.

"After dinner, then," Mary said, ascending the stairs. The junior sleuths waited a minute for Nellie to leave the lobby before following Mary to her room.

"Now, tell me," Mary said as she sat at her dressing table, removing her jewelry.

Eventually, Mary summarized the deluge of information that followed her question. "Okay, okay, so, you've found a motive of anger or revenge. Is that right?"

"Yes," Margie said breathlessly. "Constable Watkins has been having a long-running quarrel with Mr. Beacham over some investment Beacham had advised, and he'd made. Watkins accused him of theft and threatened him with arrest if the money wasn't returned."

"It's a new lead, certainly, so well done," Mary said. "Now what about Mr. Illingsworth?"

Again, a babble of words flowed from all three as they each strove to tell the story in their own unique way.

"Please, not all at once!" she exclaimed.

"Let me speak, it's my house," Margie demanded, and Winnie and Dotty quieted.

"We asked Detective Sergeant Reynolds what was going on, and he said, 'Mr. Illingsworth is helping the police with their inquiries.' He wouldn't say any more, though we pressed him pretty hard."

"Yeah, we did!" Dotty chimed in.

"But," Winnie burst in, unable to contain herself any longer,

"Mrs. Illingsworth says he's guilty and the police will get it out of him."

"Did she tell *you* that?" Mary asked, surprised a woman like Rose Illingsworth would confide in three teenage girls.

"No," Dotty admitted. "It's what their housekeeper heard her saying on the phone to an unknown friend."

Mary smiled. The village telegraph system was better than any news service. "If it's gossip, it must be true." She chuckled.

"It's true," Dotty said. "This was more than just helping them with inquiries. They had him in handcuffs, and they'd never do that if they didn't believe him guilty."

Mary frowned, puzzled, but before she could say more, Winnie jumped in. "It's because of the weedkiller they found at the Illingsworths' house. It was the right kind." She paused. "The kind of poison that killed Mr. Beacham."

"Ours was the wrong kind," Margie added, maintaining her family's innocence.

"I see, but they didn't take Mrs. Illingsworth?"

"No," Dotty replied. "Why would she kill her true love?"

"Did she say that too?"

"No." Margie shook her head. "Her maid said that. She says Mrs. Illingsworth wanted to run away with Mr. Beacham and that's why Mr. Illingsworth killed him. She's the one with the money, you see."

"But not enough," Winnie added, and Margie stuck her tongue out at her friend. This was obviously an argument they'd been having, and not yet resolved, before Mary arrived back from London.

"I fear you may have stolen Cook's thunder. She was supposed to be hearing the servants' information. Not you."

"Oh." Margie frowned. "She'll still have plenty to tell you, I'm sure. This village has been a hotbed of illicit affairs for years, and I knew nothing about it. I do think that's unfair. I'm old enough to know things like that now."

"But you weren't always old enough to know," Mary reminded her.

"I do hope my neighbors are equally interesting when I learn about them," Winnie said. "Well, *I'm* old enough to know, and I'm not going back to school or university."

"Well," Dotty said. "I hope my family's friends and neighbors aren't. That kind of thing is all very well in books or films, or here in Upper Wainbury, but it's . . ." She paused, searching for the right word. "Well, undignified. How will Margie ever look them in the face again without giggling?"

Mary grinned. "It does take some practice. Now, I must get changed or your mum will suspect something's happening without her knowledge, Margie."

"And we have to dress for country dancing," Margie added as the girls flitted out of the room. "I know we're supposed to look down on this sort of thing, but I love it. I'm going to marry a farmer and keep horses."

Mary shook her head, smiling. *So typical of a young lady of that age to have no idea what will bring them happiness.*

FIFTEEN MINUTES LATER, Mary joined Nellie in the drawing room. "Is Gerry out tonight?"

"Conservative Club board meeting," Nellie said tersely, leaving Mary to deduce there was more to this than just resentment at being left alone.

"Good," Mary said. "Because I have some questions for you that are better asked with him out of the way." She sat in an armchair directly across from Nellie, where she could study the woman's reaction to what she had to say to her.

"You were going to leave this to the police, remember?" Nellie replied.

"I said the girls should," Mary countered, "not me. How long have you known Beacham, and how long has Gerry known him?"

"Oh, you've dug that up, have you?" Nellie rose to her feet. "All right. Gerry knew the man in Germany at the end of the war. It doesn't mean he was involved with any of Beacham's criminal dealings." Nellie paced the room.

"So Beacham was involved in smuggling looted art out of Germany at the end of the war?"

"I don't know, and Gerry says he doesn't either." She threw her arms into the air. "Gerry didn't like Beacham, to be honest, but in a small place like this you have to get along with your neighbors." Nellie sat in her seat again and crossed her legs, regaining her dignity.

"If people like you had snubbed him, others would too," Mary suggested.

"First, we would have to explain why, and as I've just said, we don't know if any of what is rumored is actually true," Nellie replied. "And secondly, to announce that would've invited others to go snooping, and they'd find out Gerry knew Beacham then, and they'd say 'no smoke without fire.' We'd ourselves be shunned. Lately, Gerry has been looking for a place to buy away from here. Secretly, of course."

"Or is he just trying to escape?" Mary mused, and then reddened as she realized she'd said that aloud.

"Mary, you're supposed to be our friend."

"I am, but you must understand if *I* found this out in one day, the police will soon learn of it also. We need to have this explained and Gerry cleared by the time they arrive in force."

"There's nothing to explain. Gerry was stationed at the same place Beacham was in Berlin in 1945 and '46. Gerry was an infantry major, Beacham a sergeant in the Supply Division with a finger in every pie. They only met when something went wrong in supplies to Gerry's division, and even then it was only official business. Then, when Gerry had made enough fuss to rouse the top brass, he was asked to investigate Beacham's goings-on."

"So they were on the opposite sides of the fence?" Mary studied Nellie. "Why might people think they were in league together?"

Nellie leaned forward, her expression earnest. "Because Gerry's investigation couldn't prove any wrongdoing on Beacham's part. Everybody by then was convinced of Beacham's guilt, and in their minds, Gerry's investigation let him off the hook."

Nellie's hands outlined the trajectory of that pivotal moment, and her fingers drew an invisible line depicting Beacham's journey. "Beacham was shipped back to England at the end of the investigation, escaped prosecution, and without an official stain on his character. Gerry, however, was under a cloud of suspicion until the day he left the army." She crossed her arms. "It was terribly unfair."

Barkley trotted into the room, smelling of honey and biscuits, and lay beside Mary's feet with a loud sigh. *Been sneaking treats from the cooks again, I smell.*

"I see," Mary said sympathetically. And she did. She understood how someone as fundamentally decent and honest as Gerry could fail to catch a man everyone knew to be a crook. Poor Gerry. A task he'd take on because it was his duty, but Mary couldn't imagine a man less likely to get to the bottom of a clever thief's organization. Gerry wasn't stupid, in fact he was an intelligent, bookish man, just not a clever one when it came to people or motives.

She shook her head to clear her thoughts. "And then Beacham came to live here. Do you think that was a coincidence?"

"I doubt it. You can imagine how Gerry took his arrival. I didn't understand what he was angry about until he told me. Beacham, of course, was innocence personified, never once alluding to their shared history but always ready with the faintest of hints he might, if Gerry didn't play along with him. It's been a nightmare."

"What changed to make Gerry suddenly decide to move house?"

"He got two anonymous letters," Nellie said. "They didn't ask for money, but they made it clear they might. Gerry thought they came from Beacham and confronted him about it a month ago."

"Beacham denied it, of course?" Mary asked.

"Yes, but Gerry didn't believe him. Gerry had heard rumors Beacham's business was in trouble and therefore he wanted money."

"And then what happened?" Mary asked when it was clear Nellie might not continue.

"Well, nothing. Gerry was angry, but there wasn't anything he could do because going to the authorities would dig up the whole sordid business again."

"If Gerry is as innocent as you say, wouldn't having it investigated properly be to his benefit? This time he could be shown to be innocent."

"Easy for you to say, Mary," Nellie snapped. "It's easier to prove someone guilty than to prove them innocent. Think about it. What happened was thirteen years ago in another country. Everyone involved is scattered by this time. There'd be no conclusion that would prove Gerry did nothing wrong, only more of the same whispered lies like last time."

"I understand, only you must recognize it will soon come to light and in the worst possible way. Now it's a motive for murder."

"There are more motives than this one."

"Yes, there are," Mary agreed. "And the police will find and investigate all of them. I fear this is the one that will catch the eye of the press and the public. It has everything: corruption by senior people, wartime smuggling, black market dealing, blackmail, and murder. It's a novel waiting to be written."

"You're one of our oldest friends, Mary," Nellie cried. "You have to prove it untrue before it gets out into the press."

Oh, now I have to save the day, when just yesterday I was to leave it to the police. Mary said, "I'll do everything I can, but Gerry must tell me honestly what happened then and what has happened now."

"I'll make him," Nellie said. "The moment he's home."

10

DOUBLES DISCOVERY

Gerry was home so late, it was the following morning before Mary was able to speak to him alone, which she did when she entered the breakfast room.

"Gerry."

He cut her short. "Nellie told me. We can talk, but let's walk away from the house. I don't want the girls or the servants to hear any of this."

Mary, Nellie and Gerry set out to wander the footpaths behind the Marmalades' manor. They were soon among fields of ripening wheat and well out of the village, though they could still hear the busyness of the new road.

"Now," Gerry said, puffing on his pipe, "you can ask your questions, and I'll answer them honestly."

"It would be best for you to tell your story," Mary said. "But perhaps my questions will serve as a starting point. Back in Berlin, were you in any way involved with Beacham and his dealings?"

"Absolutely not! Nasty little tick. I wouldn't have any dealings with him of any kind. I'd as soon not invite him to the house, but Nellie would say people will talk if we don't."

"And so they would," Nellie grumbled. "And we'd have to say why."

"Yes, yes," Gerry said testily, his lips puckering on the bit of his pipe. "The only involvement in Berlin was me being asked to lead the investigation into his dealings."

"And you found no wrongdoing?"

Gerry frowned and pulled his pipe to speak clearly. "We didn't, but I suspected that was because too many people were in on it and they stymied every line of inquiry we followed."

"Are you in touch with anyone from that time?"

Gerry shook his head. "I was pretty well frozen out by the end. They didn't even arrange a leaving-do for me. That's how bad it was."

"Did you raise your concerns with the senior officers at the time?"

With his hand on the bowl of his pipe, Gerry paced a circle in the field while Mary stood to the side in a clearing, keeping a watchful eye on the pair.

"I did, which is why things escalated. Somehow, my complaint got out, and that was that. There was no follow-up, except my transfer home."

"And when you received the letters?"

"I saw at once who they were from," Gerry said. "He didn't try to hide it. Only someone who knew about Berlin in '45 could have known. And the writer used phrases Beacham regularly used. It had to be him."

"You confronted him?"

Gerry stopped and tamped down the tobacco to extinguish it. "Of course. He was risking both our standings in the community with this act of stupidity."

Mary sighed. Gerry was as unhelpful as Nellie had been. "Tell me what happened, what was said, what you both did—tell me everything." Mary raised her voice as high as she dared.

"We said a lot of things," Gerry replied, running his hand through his hair. "I can't remember it all. He did say the reason I couldn't get anything on him in Germany was because he hadn't done anything wrong, which I'm sure was a lie. It made me even angrier."

More motive to kill? Mary stepped farther away.

"What did he say about the letters?" Mary's frustration rose.

"He said he hadn't sent them, but the person sending letters to him had. I asked who that was. He didn't know, but that's rot. If it wasn't him, he must've known who it was—they knew how he spoke, as well as everything about him."

"He had no suggestions? His business partner, perhaps?"

"He was confident it wasn't his partner," Gerry replied.

Mary changed tack. "What about his wife?"

"You can't think Fran would do this?" Gerry asked. "She couldn't know all the background."

Really? No wonder Gerry didn't catch Beacham. One of the most obvious suspects and he just won't see it.

Mary sighed. "How long was she married to Cyril?"

"Eight years," Nellie replied. "More than long enough to listen, learn, and plot."

"I don't believe it!" Gerry cried. "Fran's a wonderful woman. How she put up with Cyril all these years I don't know."

"Maybe because she'd found her ticket out," Mary responded sarcastically. "I take it you didn't ask him if he believed it was Fran?"

"Of course I didn't. The whole idea is preposterous."

Mary shook her head in frustration. Gerry wore blinders when it came to people, and probably women in particular.

"Did he have anything to say that might help us now?"

Gerry huffed. "Nothing. I told you. He just denied everything."

"Very well, was there anything about the letters you recognized beyond the phrases Cyril would use?"

Gerry shook his head.

"Do you still have them?"

"I burned them in case they were seen by the servants." He shrugged.

"Did *you* see them, Nellie?"

"No. They made Gerry so angry he stormed out to confront Cyril the moment they arrived. I didn't even know about the first one until Gerry came back from that meeting."

"What can you remember about them?" Mary asked Gerry.

"They were posted in London, two different postal districts, I think. They were typed on plain paper."

"What did they say exactly?" Mary continued. He had to remember something about them. Nothing that made a person angry enough to confront someone was easily forgotten.

"That the writer knew what Beacham and I were up to in Berlin and didn't I think it was time I shared some of the profits."

"Did they say why they were writing now, after all these years?"

"No, nothing like that," Gerry responded tersely.

"Have you sold any art or other collectibles recently that may have triggered this? Anything that got into the newspapers, for instance?"

Gerry and Nellie spoke in unison. Gerry said, "No." But Nellie said, "Yes."

Mary frowned. "Which is it?"

"It didn't get into the newspapers," Nellie said. "But we did recently sell a painting. We needed the money to repair the roof."

"But that painting was in my family for generations," Gerry argued "It wasn't something I acquired in my lifetime."

"Maybe the writer didn't know that," Mary speculated.

"Maybe they've been waiting for the moment you sold something and assumed what you sold was an item you and Beacham smuggled out of Germany."

He tugged at his collar. "That assumes they were around all those years ago, either in Germany, or maybe just in the army." He paused, glaring at Nellie. "Or maybe here at home but heard all the talk and listened because they knew me. If so, that's a long list of suspects."

"Maybe we can narrow it down," Mary said. "Spend some time thinking about it. It must be someone who remembers that time, or has heard about it, and knows where you live. You aren't a public figure whose name and address is widely known."

"It's impossible," Gerry declared.

"We'll start immediately." Nellie sidled up to her husband. "I can think of two names already."

"Who?" Gerry looked at her quizzically.

"We'll sit in the library and work on it," Nellie said. "Now!"

Grumbling, Gerry followed her back to the house, still maintaining it couldn't be done.

Mary shook her head. More and more she understood how Beacham, and his accomplices, and higher-ups, had bamboozled Gerry and his investigation all those years ago. *Can I entirely trust any list Nellie collates? She has her own motives for getting rid of Beacham and pointing the finger elsewhere. If Beacham was threatening her family, either because of the blackmail or because he and she were at some point lovers, Nellie was the kind of person who would act to stop the problem. Did she have the opportunity?*

Mary was still deciding if she should return to the house with Nellie and Gerry or finish what could be an enjoyable stroll, when the three young ladies headed straight for her.

"We looked all over for you," Margie cried. "Lucky for us, Ponsonby knew where you'd be."

Lucky for me.

"Lucky for all of us, you're awake already," Mary agreed, with an earnest smile. "Because I have a new task for you three."

"We haven't told you about the Agricultural Show's country dance yet," Winnie said. "And what we learned there."

"I'm pleased to hear you weren't there just enjoying yourselves," Mary said playfully as they walked back toward the manor.

"Well, we didn't," Dotty responded with a hint of exaggeration. "Enjoy ourselves, I mean."

"Speak for yourself, Dotty," Margie teased with a mischievous twinkle in her eye. "Just because the boy you liked danced all night with his fiancée doesn't mean the rest of us were unhappy."

Mary swiftly intervened, defusing the brewing banter. "Is this how you came to learn something new, Dotty?"

Dotty's smile turned smug. "Yes, it is. I now know we can stop considering Constable Watkins. His wife was serving at the bar, and she told me the constable had made it clear to Beacham the police would look into his, Beacham's, affairs if he, Watkins, didn't get his money back."

"And he got it back?"

"He did. Mr. Beacham didn't fancy the police investigating him," Winnie replied. "Don't you think that's significant?"

Mary contemplated for a moment. "Maybe, but it puzzles me why Beacham should try to get money from a policeman in the first place? Particularly if he was going to defraud him."

Margie agreed, "It's odd, but I think Mr. Beacham was the sort of man who thought he could swindle anyone *and* get away with it. He had that air about him. You know, confidence and mischief and . . ." She trailed off. "Well, I don't know quite how to explain it, but I think he'd view it as a great triumph to swindle the local bobby out of his savings."

Rubbing the back of her neck, Mary sighed, resigned. "From all I've heard, he does seem that kind of man."

"What was it you wanted us to do, Lady Mary?" Dotty asked.

"I want to know how Beacham came to the party," Mary said. "Everyone else we know had car trouble; they mentioned it. Did the Beachams?"

"That's a bit dull." Winnie rolled her eyes.

"It's possible Beacham was poisoned before he arrived at the party. The police are looking at nicotine-based products, but nicotine poisoning isn't instant. In fact, it can take hours to kill someone."

"So we should snoop in his garden shed too." Winnie brightened.

Dotty shook her head. "The police looked there. I discovered that last night too."

"Your evening was not wasted, Dotty," Mary said. "Well done. We knew about the Illingsworths' garden shed, but Beacham's own house we didn't."

"We could have guessed." Margie rocked on her heels. "After all, they must have Fran in the frame, as they say in the detective movies."

"True, but now we're more certain," Mary said. "So, how did the Beachams travel to your house, Margie? Did they stop anywhere along the way, the pub maybe? Was Beacham drinking before he left his house or along the way from his hip flask? Anything else you can discover, we need to know."

They stopped so Dotty could take notes. Dotty flipped the page in her small pad and wrote furiously. Glancing up, she asked, "Should we ask about everything he did, ate and drank from the moment he got up that morning until he arrived at the Marmalade house?"

Mary beamed with satisfaction. "Yes, that's it."

On cue, Barkley bounded out of the house toward Mary, skittering across the drive. "What have you been getting up to?" Mary asked the plump corgi as she bent and stroked his matted fur. "You're all sticky."

She straightened. "Okay, ladies, gather all the information. Nothing skipped. I'm afraid Barkley needs bathing, and that will take me some time."

"I'll take care of it," Dotty cooed.

"That's lovely, dear. Please do. I appreciate it," Mary replied. *One of the perks of being a duchess is people always want to do your work for you. They feel duchesses, or any aristocracy, shouldn't do manual labor. It's a lovely hangover from the Middle Ages.*

"Only Mrs. Beacham can answer some of those," Margie said, refocusing on the case. "And I don't know how happy she'll be at our questioning."

With a conspiratorial gleam in her eye, Mary said, "Oh, you mustn't *question* her. You just talk to her. If you get it right, she'll tell you exactly what you want to know."

Margie's eyebrows rose in intrigue. "We previously wondered about our servants," she said hesitantly. "Our parlor maid is a very pretty woman, and whenever he visited, Mr. Beacham always made comments about it directly to her. Our housekeeper didn't like it; she's very protective of the female staff."

"As she should be." Mary nodded. "I hope Cook will bring me all we need to know from that side of the household very soon."

She shooed them into the house, and the girls tottered off with the dog, noisily planning what they would say to get Fran Beacham talking. Winnie protested being involved in Barkley's bath time.

"Oh, Winnie," Dotty said. "Do stop complaining. Taking

Barkley on our investigations will provide lots of opportunities to talk with the villagers. You'll see."

UPSTAIRS IN HER ROOM, Mary rang the service bell. Ponsonby appeared, answering her summons before the bell's chimes had stopped ringing.

"Your Grace?"

"Would you please ask Cook to come and see me, Ponsonby, and you too. We have some catching up to do and then some next steps to consider."

Cook followed Ponsonby in just moments later with a fresh basket of buttered scones, local butter and strawberry jam. As they nibbled, Cook told them what she'd learned while they had been in London, including about the friction between the Marmalades' housekeeper and Cyril Beacham.

"Margie has heard that too," Mary agreed.

"It warrants investigating, milady," Cook said. "I'll keep digging there, if you agree."

"I do. Now, what do we know of the Beachams?"

Here Cook flashed Mary a puzzled expression. "The staff say Mrs. Beacham tolerated her husband's affairs, suggesting she was happy it meant she was left alone. I can't believe anyone would be so unconcerned, though it's true the money in the family is mainly hers."

Barkley trotted into the room. "I see you've had your bath, sir." Mary petted him, and then shook the wetness from her hand. The girls didn't dry him off very well.

Mary put her feet atop the ottoman and leaned back in the chair. "Mr. Beacham's business hasn't gone well?"

"I understand the running expenses were all his, if you catch my drift, but their wealth was hers, if the business failed. The staff know this because there were twice delays in their salaries being paid, and Mrs. Beacham stepped in to cover the shortfall."

"Was this recently?"

"In the last year, yes," Cook said.

"And the Illingsworths?"

"Oh, what I learned explains exactly why the police arrested him." Cook waved her hands animatedly.

Mary guessed, "They quarreled over the affair?"

"Often," Cook replied. "In public they may have put on brave faces, but Mr. Illingsworth was growing increasingly angry. The affair was becoming known around the village, you see."

"And he found that humiliating," Mary mused, rocking in the chair.

"Well, anyone would, wouldn't they?" Cook tucked a stray hair into her cap.

"Yes, I imagine so. Were there threats spoken?"

"By Mr. Illingsworth, yes. His threats weren't toward his wife, though, just against Mr. Beacham."

Mary frowned. "Did you learn the nature of these threats? Illingsworth was a much bigger man than Beacham. I would expect him to say he'd punch him, not poison him."

Cook straightened, her uniform crisp. "Well, they do say he made several threats, and that's what the police picked up on."

"Then we need to know if there's any way Illingsworth could have put poison in anything Beacham ate or drank that morning," Mary suggested. "Did they arrive at the same time, maybe, and was there some moment that gave him the opportunity?"

"I'll ask, milady, but it's not likely, not if the poison was in the hip flask."

"Well, we don't yet know for certain it was," Mary replied. "I presumed it might be, and the police have said he was poisoned."

"I believe, my lady," said Ponsonby, who'd remained silent while Cook relayed the results of her investigations to Mary, "we may hear the results of the postmortem tomorrow."

"That will help a lot. We're spreading our information-gathering over a wide range right now, perhaps too wide, and it would be good to narrow things down." She paused. "Cook, do you remember anything being said by the Illingsworths' or Marmalades' cooks that may be productive?"

"No, milady," Cook said. "Why?"

"It was just a thought. If the Illingsworth household was being upset by what was happening, could their cook have been encouraged by Mr. Illingsworth to do something she maybe didn't realize she was doing?"

Frowning, Cook said, "I can't imagine any cook doing anything of the sort, but the Illingsworths' cook, Mrs. Yelland, isn't the persuadable sort."

"I'm glad to hear that," Mary said. "Your recommendation of her goes a long way with me. However, if he was poisoned in food or drink, I would expect the cooks and servers to have some inkling how it was done. I feel your avenue of inquiry is one that could carry us the furthest in solving this case. Keep going."

Cook beamed with pride. Her role being considered more important than her rival Ponsonby's was something she would never forget.

"I will, milady, have no fear. I too still think there's more to learn from them. Beacham's own cook, Miss Harbottle, for instance, is very reticent about her schedule that morning."

"Do none of the others shed any light on her movements?"

"Only that she arrived later than the others," Cook replied. "But also she's a hard worker and soon made up for it."

"Find out what you can." Mary smiled. "I expect she was busy and just lost track of the time. We all know how that is."

"Likely that's so, milady. Still, I'll dig a little deeper there, to be sure."

And how do I dig deeper into Nellie's activities? I can't use any of my Society comrades to investigate. If it's Nellie, it will destroy Margie and Gerry and devastate me. And I am not finished with the cooks either; could Mrs. Yelland's loyalty be her undoing? Is Miss Harbottle's being late that morning significant?

11

CROSSCOURT CLUES

As always, Ponsonby's information was spot-on. Inspector Acton, along with Sergeant Reynolds, arrived at the Marmalade home early the following morning, calling everyone to the incident room for the preliminary postmortem report. While the inspector didn't provide it to the family or Lady Mary to read, his questions pointed to certain details.

He wanted to know, once again, what everyone had eaten, had anyone seen Beacham eat or drink anything earlier the others didn't, and so on.

"Does this mean the hip flask was not the source of the poison?" Mary asked.

"We have reason to believe it wasn't from anything he drank or ate at the party," Acton said. "Perhaps earlier."

"Unfortunately, none of us saw Mr. Beacham before he arrived at the party," Nellie said. "I think that's right, isn't it?" She glanced at the girls and Mary.

Everyone nodded as Acton eyed each in turn. He didn't appear convinced.

"His wife would be the best person to answer that question, Inspector, surely?" Nellie suggested.

"Beacham was out most of the morning before returning home to change before your party," Acton said. "Mrs. Beacham said he wouldn't say where. So, I repeat, did any of you see him that morning?"

Again, everyone answered no, shaking their heads.

"I suggest you talk to Mrs. Illingsworth," Mary said.

"We intend to. I hoped someone who had less reason to lie may have seen him," he muttered, and with that, he and Reynolds quickly left.

There was a brief silence before Gerry said, "Looks like we're in the clear, then."

Nellie glared at him. "Hadn't the fact we didn't kill him put us in the clear already, Gerry?"

He laughed. "He wouldn't take our word for it, so not in Acton's eyes we weren't."

"Gerry's right, Nellie," Mary said. "Finally, it looks to the police like you and your staff were not involved."

"That would rule out two of the Illingsworths' servants too," Margie said. "Their cook and a maid were here helping out that day, and so was the Beachams' cook, Janet Harbottle."

"Very true," said Mary. "Though we can't entirely rule out the servants."

"I think it puts the servants back on the list," Winnie said thoughtfully. "They couldn't put poison in his hip flask but could put it in something only he ate or drank. Was there anything like that?"

No one knew the answer to that. "We need to find out," Winnie said.

"Cook can help there," Mary offered. "She's been trading recipes and secrets with the other cooks. She could ask that question without raising suspicions."

"I'll ask our cook as well," Nellie added.

Mary shook her head. "That would alert the servants we are

now suspecting them and we don't want that. It's still highly unlikely they could poison something and be sure only Beacham would eat it."

With this agreed, the group broke up and went to their chosen occupations of the morning. For the girls and Mary, that meant another meeting away from Nellie. Mary led the way into the garden and out of sight of the house.

"If they haven't already," Mary began, "the police will likely realize Beacham may have been injected with poison. If so, the police surgeon will now be looking for a puncture mark."

"He would've noticed if he'd been injected, wouldn't he?" Dotty asked. "Injections hurt."

"You're a baby," Winnie sassed. "If it's done right, they hardly hurt at all."

"Yes, but if it was being done secretly, there wouldn't be any opportunity to do it right," Dotty replied hotly.

"And he might have been asleep," Margie said. "Or doing something in the garden and been stung by a wasp or bee. Maybe he had allergies?"

Mary said, "All good ideas. Now how do we find out where he was that morning?"

"We go and ask," Winnie said. "Someone in the village must have seen him walking to or from wherever it was."

"That's right." Mary smiled. "Now, go."

"What will you be doing?" Margie asked.

"Ponsonby and I will be sleuthing on our own," Mary replied cryptically.

When her sleuthing assistants were gone, Mary strolled back to the house and headed up to her room. She rang the bell for Ponsonby, who was at her side so quickly, he could only have been waiting outside the door.

"Ah, Ponsonby," Mary said. "We've just learned the hip flask wasn't how the poison was delivered. Nor is it likely it was in the food served at the party. Cook has the inside track on the cooks and the servers that day in case there's something there, and the girls are finding out where Beacham was that morning. And let's check in with Gerry before you're off to London tomorrow. "

Having sent all the girls out to work the case, Mary and Ponsonby walked to the library, where Gerry and Nellie had returned to their task which also included more arguing about who should, and who shouldn't, be on the list.

Barkley sat at the center of it, his head volleying back and forth with the discussion. Mary petted him. "You're nice and soft after your bath, now that you're dry. I'm sure you enjoyed the attention."

"Have you agreed on any names?" Mary asked.

"No!" Gerry said emphatically and drew from his pipe.

"Gerry means he won't agree to the names I suggest," Nellie said.

"Because these people are old friends and colleagues. I won't set them up to be treated like criminals."

"Not like criminals, Gerry," Mary said, "like witnesses."

Gerry settled down. He considered the idea for a moment. "We talk to them ourselves, and we don't involve the police?"

"We won't involve the police unless something from our interviews suggests criminal behavior," Mary said, in what she hoped was a reassuring tone.

"Very well," Gerry said. "The two people Nellie mentioned—my old batman, Corporal Foreman, and my fellow officer on the investigation, Major Lennox. We've kept in touch over the years, only Christmas and the like, but they're the only two I believe know where I am and know of the events of 1945 and '46. But they were with me at the time. They know I wasn't stealing artwork."

"I'm sure you're right," Mary replied to Gerry. "But people's circumstances change. I'll speak to Major Lennox as soon as possible, while Ponsonby finds and talks to Corporal Foreman."

Mary and Ponsonby left the still squabbling Gerry and Nellie and closed the door behind them. Confident they were safe to talk, Mary said to Ponsonby, "We should have some more background by tomorrow when you travel to London to meet with Mr. Marmalade's old army pal and I will have contacted the other one. Gerry says they're not involved, but even if he's right, I wonder what more they can tell us about Beacham and that failed investigation."

When Ponsonby left, Mary pondered while freshening up and tidying her hair. *We have information leading to a number of motives: business, especially those gangsters; sexual, a jealous husband perhaps; or a blackmail victim's revenge. Is there an unknown motive that we haven't discovered yet? And if so, does that mean there's a suspect X we haven't yet identified? Maybe Lennox or Foreman will come up trumps for us?*

12

A TANGLED MATCH

Later that day, Mary's bedroom once again provided the quiet haven where the trio of Mary, Ponsonby, and Cook gathered for a confidential briefing. Seated at a desk, Mary composed her posture. Nearby, Ponsonby stood attentive. Cook entered the room with a purposeful stride.

Mary outlined the tasks she wanted them to do: Cook to discover if someone could poison just Beacham's food, and Ponsonby to find and interview Corporal Foreman. "Do you have any questions?"

"Not so much a question, milady, as a comment," Cook said promptly, before Ponsonby could speak. "I wasn't with the others that day as they prepared the food for the tennis party." She removed her cap, fussing with it before replacing it atop her head, exactly the way it was previously. "But speaking to those who were, I don't believe any of them could have put something in the food or drinks and be sure only Mr. Beacham would take it."

Mary nodded in understanding, already processing the implications of Cook's observation. "I think you're right. But we have to consider the possibility." Her fingers tapped lightly against the desk, a quiet rhythm of contemplation. "For example, was there something Mr. Beacham particularly liked that no one else did?"

"I'll ask," Cook assured her. "His cook, Miss Harbottle, was there. She would know."

Barkley entered the room, his tail wagging in excited greeting.

"Don't be too obvious with Miss Harbottle," Mary added. Barkley perked up his ears as if understanding the nature of the discussion. "Remember, we're just interested observers here. We don't want anyone suspecting we're investigating, or Inspector Acton will be down on us like a ton of bricks."

Ponsonby, seizing the moment, interjected. "Mine is something of an observation too. While I'm in London, meeting with Corporal Foreman, it may be wise for me to stay overnight and finally establish if Beacham's partner owns a motorcycle or not."

Amid this exchange, Cook picked up a nearby vase and began arranging the flowers.

Mary's response was swift and decisive. "Very well. Phone me tomorrow evening after you've watched him and confirmed the answer one way or another."

Barkley trotted over to Cook with an air of curiosity and nudged her leg, seeking a friendly pat. She obliged and then nonchalantly wiped the fur off her stocking. "You need a good brushing, my lad," she muttered under her breath while Mary and Ponsonby continued speaking.

"I hope," Ponsonby said, "there'll be a train this afternoon which will get me into London today, before he closes the gallery. That way, I'll have that confirmed this evening."

Mary sent them both on their way and went downstairs, reluctantly, for she was very aware of the danger of what she was about to do—putting her old friends, Gerry and Nellie, in grave danger of prison *and* social ruin. When she was sure she wasn't being observed, she knocked gently on the police incident room door. A constable opened it, and Mary asked to speak to Inspector Acton. The man looked back into the room and, getting a positive response, let Mary in.

"Inspector," Mary said. "I've learned something about Mr. Beacham I think you should know."

He motioned her to a seat. "What is it?"

"In Berlin, 1945, Beacham worked in the army quartermaster division, and he was suspected of dealing in looted artwork. He was investigated, and nothing was proven, but he was shipped back to Britain quickly after, so there may have been something to it."

"And you think this may have something to do with why he was killed?"

"I'm of two minds about it. I just wanted you to know it might not be about shady dealings in today's art world," Mary said.

"Certainly no one in Upper Wainbury has mentioned this possibility, so thanks for the information. I don't think it's a strong motive, though."

"As I said, Inspector, I'm torn between thinking there's a link and thinking it's all too long ago. You may do with it as you please."

"I'll have the London boys check with the army records people," Acton said. "If he wasn't charged then, I can't see anyone being concerned enough now to kill him."

"Unless one of his accomplices back then saw something that made them realize they were cheated and Beacham chose to bluff it out instead of making amends," Mary suggested.

"Anything's possible," Acton said, smiling. "And we'll follow it up. I promise."

Mary was escorted to the door, where she once again

ensured her visit to the police was not being observed before exiting the room.

WITH HER TWO TRUSTED COMPANIONS, Cook and Ponsonby, gone to fulfill their allotted tasks, and her unpleasant duty of snitching performed, Mary went into the village, searching for the girls, leaving Barkley at the manor.

I hope they'll have some information on Beacham's whereabouts that morning. Something strong enough to persuade me Gerry isn't involved. She found them in the Bluebell Café, Upper Wainbury's only teashop, eating scones smothered in double cream and strawberry jam.

"You're rebuilding your energy with Devonshire cream teas, I see," Mary teased. "This must mean your investigations have gone well." She sat in an empty seat.

Dotty, the only one between bites, replied, "We're celebrating."

Mary cocked her head, waiting for the reason.

Dotty stared past Mary's head, a trait that had Mary wondering if Dotty had a touch of extrasensory perception.

"Where was Beacham, then?"

Margie licked her jammy fingers. "That we haven't found out yet, but we do know he came from the direction of the village and not from the direction of his house." She licked the remaining sweetness from her lips. "Finding the actual place will be a doddle."

Puzzled, Mary asked, "He came from the village? Did he have friends, or a friend, there? And why go that morning, when he knew he was expected at the tennis tournament by ten o'clock? He must have left home early, already dressed for tennis. Doesn't that seem odd?"

Winnie shrugged. "He might have gone to post a letter or pay a bill. We'll know soon enough." She wiped her mouth carefully with a napkin. "There's nowhere to hide in the village."

"Congratulations, ladies," Mary said, feeling encouragement was due. "With persistence, we shall soon have the full story. But we must leave the teashop if we are to continue the investigation."

Dotty smiled sheepishly.

The walk back to the manor was as silent as Mary had ever known from the girls. *They all have tummy aches,* she guessed. *That'll teach them to overload on sweets.* They spoke to passersby in the street as they walked, but no further information was discovered about where Beacham had spent the hours between leaving his house and arriving at the Marmalades'.

That's certainly odd. How could he not be seen? Mary contemplated all the people the young sleuths had spoken with, knocked on so many doors without success. *Maybe he didn't go into the village but took a route that avoided the village? Arriving at the Marmalades' house from a direction that looked like he came from the village? Is that possible? And if he didn't come from there, then where did he go that day?*

Brushing Barkley, Dotty unwittingly agreed with Mary's unspoken sentiment. "It's odd no one saw him come into the village that morning. No one admitted to being outside at the time, but still, people usually look out windows."

"It was the weekend," Winnie said, sitting in the wingback chair, crossing her legs and inspecting her nails. "Many sleep late on the weekends."

"Are there any abandoned buildings?" Mary asked. "Somewhere he might go to meet a lover, perhaps?"

"Only old sheds," Dotty replied. Barkley, sitting obediently as she brushed through his double coat of fur, suddenly leapt to his feet as if expecting to be immediately investigating old sheds. "Would Beacham risk messing up his clothes before appearing at the Marmalades' tennis party?"

Mary and Winnie both silently shook their heads.

"I expect you're right, but we should search for them, in case," Mary encouraged.

"Tomorrow," Margie replied. "I'm worn out from walking the beat and sleuthing all day." She slumped onto the love seat nearest Mary.

"You shouldn't have had so many cream teas." Mary smiled.

"We didn't overdo it," Dotty said, but Barkley licked her cheek to prove otherwise. "In the afternoon it helped boost our energy. I should've had the macaroon as well."

Ignoring Dotty's desire for cakes, Mary said, "I spoke to Cook when she returned from interviewing her fellow professionals, and she too had no new information to share. The cooks all agreed; nothing was prepared especially for Mr. Beacham, and every one of them had a hand in preparing all the food." *This was a most frustrating day. I couldn't make contact with Major Lennox, the girls couldn't find where Beacham was for the time before arriving here at the house, and the cooks ruled out any possible food source of poison at the party.* "I hope Ponsonby has some good news when he phones later."

Entering on cue, as Ponsonby would likely have done, Cook replied, "I'm sure he'll present you with good news, milady. You know what men are like. May I get you some tea?"

Mary shook her head and the phone trilled.

"Speaking of," Cook turned quickly and took it upon herself to answer the Marmalades' phone. "For you, milady. It's Ponsonby." She grinned as if she'd orchestrated the precise timing of the call.

Ponsonby did have good news. "Winkler has a Brough Superior motorcycle, a classic machine much desired by collectors throughout the country."

"So he could have been our mystery motorcyclist," Mary replied.

"I think it's very likely, my lady. The Superior is guaranteed to do one hundred miles per hour, and while the roads near Upper Wainbury aren't conducive to those speeds, the new road nearby, and those now radiating out from London, would make it a swift journey."

"If it was Winkler burgling Beacham's house, whatever he was looking for must've been important," Mary mused. "It was risky. Driving down here in the evening after the gallery closed, burgling the house after everyone was in bed, and then driving back to London through the night to be ready for opening the gallery that morning."

"Quite so, my lady. And there's another thing to consider. To buy such a classic machine today is extremely expensive. I suggest far more than the part-owner of the gallery in London could afford, no matter how expensive their art is."

Mary smiled. "Perhaps not so difficult if their art and antiques are as fraudulent as has been put forward."

"Quite so, or maybe word got around about their fakes, and it isn't as lucrative as it had been. It's possible he learned about Beacham's past life and began blackmailing his partner in the hope of taking part of his partner's share of the dwindling profits. The letters, while knowledgeable about the events, didn't provide any clues about the blackmailer."

"Maybe Beacham discovered it was Winkler and confronted him," Mary replied. "And maybe Winkler came down to murder Beacham, only he wasn't at home."

"I don't think blackmailers murder their victims, my lady. It's most often the other way around, I believe."

"You're probably right, but he came here for something. I wonder, did he find it?"

"Lady Mary," Winnie interjected excitedly. "Maybe Beacham had evidence of Winkler's wrongdoing and Winkler came for that, not to murder..." Mary hushed Winnie to listen to the telephone conversation and Cook exited with a nod.

On the phone, Ponsonby was saying, "At the time of the burglary, Beacham said nothing was taken, but maybe, now he's dead, his wife might tell us a different story."

"Yes, that's true. I'll follow up on that in the morning. Have you made contact with Corporal Foreman?"

"I had time to find his house, my lady, but he wasn't in when I rang the bell, and I couldn't wait because I wanted to spy Winkler leaving the gallery."

"And that was the right decision," Mary replied. "For now we can theorize Winkler could've been the person who burgled the Beacham house just before Beacham died."

"I'll return to Mr. Foreman's house in the morning. Have the girls heard anything about the previous strange happenings during their investigations?"

"You know, I'd forgotten about the cat and the dog." Mary cocked her head in contemplation. "They've wandered off, but I'll find them right now. They'll be in the billiard room, doing what they like to do best—"

"Pretending to be adults," they said in unison, and Mary smirked.

"Though best not to suggest anything like that to them. I recall, when I was younger, being very conscious of the need to be considered an adult," Ponsonby cautioned.

Mary chuckled. "I do too. Mum's the word. We can all convene again tomorrow after your return. Please get the earliest train you can." She ended the conversation and replaced the handset. She snapped her fingers, and Barkley was quick to her side as she went in search of her three assistants.

As she'd predicted, the girls were in the billiard room. Barkley announced their arrival with two sharp barks, and the girls immediately turned their attention to Mary.

"I have a question, ladies," Mary stated. "Something I've let slide these past days but you may have heard mention of in your interviews with the villagers. Has anyone brought up the odd incidents at all?"

Margie replied, "Only one. Mr. Quartermaine, whose dog was poisoned. He said now that there's been a human poisoning, the police might take the matter seriously. He's still very upset. Understandably."

"Nothing more?"

Dotty interjected, "He said he'd told the police at the time, the poisoner was practicing for a human victim."

"He had no thoughts on who the evildoer might be?" Mary asked, and all three shook their heads.

"Then you must ask again about the incidents," Mary said. "Not just the poisonings but the damaged cars, and anything else people may have noticed that seemed suspicious but hasn't yet been brought to our attention."

Margie groaned, Winnie nodded, and Dotty buzzed, "Yummy. More time in the Bluebell Café."

"We can't eat any more," Margie said. "Where do you even put it? You're as thin as a rail!"

"We can split our forces. I don't need the exercise." Winnie grinned. "I'll make *conversation* in the café, while you two walk the streets looking for victims—sorry, I mean witnesses."

"Very funny." Margie harrumphed. "We're not *walking the streets*, we're *walking the beat*, but we have to stick together. One of us alone could be attacked—there is a killer on the loose still. And they likely already know we're investigating."

"And to be sure I'm safe, I won't leave the café until you two return," Winnie said. "There, it's settled. We start again in the morning."

Before the objections could become heated, Mary told them the rest of Ponsonby's update.

When Mary finished speaking, Margie said, "I know Mrs. Beacham rather well. Maybe I should go and talk to her."

"Leaving me to wander the streets alone and be murdered," Dotty cried. "We go together if we're going there. Beacham's house is where the crime began, you can be sure of it."

"It's true," Mary mused. "It's where Beacham lived. It was the center of his philandering, his dodgy business dealings, and, of course, where the betrayal of his wife would be most severely felt. And you're right, Margie. Someone who knows her better than I do might get more from her than an almost stranger."

"We'll start with Mrs. Beacham in the morning." Margie leaned in, her eyes fixed on Mary. "She may actually know where her husband was that morning, only she doesn't like to say."

A faint line creased Margie's forehead. "Maybe." Her gaze shifted toward the ground for a moment. "I'm just saying she might have an idea. Family members often know more than they say."

Dotty scooted closer, eyes gleaming with curiosity. "Ooh," she purred, nudging Margie with her elbow. "Tell, tell, tell."

Heat rose to Margie's cheeks. "I was speaking generally, not specifically," she stammered, her fingers fidgeting with the hem of her blouse.

Mary slid her chair back and excused herself—leaving the young ladies to their chatter, which was thankfully fading as she distanced herself from the conversation.

THE NEXT MORNING brought a new shock to the Marmalade household. Inspector Acton arrived and invited Gerry down to the station to help the police with their inquiries.

Gerry demanded to know the reason but was silenced when Acton told him the police had learned of Gerry's confrontation with Beacham, and there had been subsequent inquiries made by the police into the background of the quarrel. They suggested Gerry pack an overnight bag, in case the inquiries went on late.

With Gerry and the police gone, the house was left in stunned silence.

"It's not true, is it, Mum?" Margie asked, breaking into the emptiness, her blonde brows knitted with worry.

Nellie took Margie's hand. "It certainly is not true." She spoke firmly. "Your father never had anything to do with Beacham's wartime get-rich-quick scheme. Unfortunately, when your father failed to find evidence of Beacham's wrongdoing, many people concluded he was in on it and had covered it up."

Dotty, sitting close by, leaned forward, her eyes wide with curiosity. "How awful. Was there nothing he could do?"

Nellie sighed, her gaze dropping. "He asked the colonel to bring in the military police and have them investigate, but the colonel wouldn't hear of it. Honor of the regiment and all that."

Winnie, always one to speak her mind, chimed in, "Hmm, my money is on the colonel as Beacham's accomplice."

Her expression grim, Mary nodded in agreement. "I'm sure Gerry and his fellow investigator also came to that conclusion, but they mustn't have uncovered anything to suggest a connection. Nellie, you ask him and ask if that colonel is still around."

Nellie agreed, but her voice didn't hide her reluctance. "He doesn't like to talk about it." Quiet, the room grew heavy before

Nellie conceded, "You're right, Mary, I'll ask him when he's released."

If he is released. I'm glad Inspector Acton kept me out of the reasons they took Gerry, but I feel this may well be the beginning of the end for him. The evidence, while not yet damning, points to Gerry. How sure am I about this? It's justice if I'm right, and a disaster if I'm wrong.

Mary ended her contemplation. "Well, he's now being investigated for murder because of this old event. The time for not *wanting* to talk about it has passed. He has no choice. He must either talk to us or the police."

What a choice. The police have the best chance to get to the truth and clear him and his name, but will they? What incentive do they have to do that? None! While I have a strong reason to do so. This would be a major disaster for Gerry and Nellie and a small disaster for me. If only I could be sure he was innocent back in 1945. How likely is it that all the senior officers in the division were in on it, except Gerry?

How will he explain the past and those letters?

13

SERVE OF SUSPICION

When her assistants left to interview Fran Beacham, Mary asked Nellie to go over everything she knew about the wartime event that might be the motive of this murder.

"There's nothing to tell," Nellie said. "I've never really known anything about it until Gerry got those letters, and even then it was a struggle to get him to talk."

"Very well," Mary said. "You heard us saying Beacham was away from his home that morning—do you have any idea where he might have been?"

"I would say with Rose Illingsworth," Nellie replied unhappily. "But it's inconceivable they would meet immediately before the tennis party. How would Rose explain her absence to Victor? Rose is a woman who likes to look her best. She takes hours to get ready. There'd be no time for her to meet with Cyril and then get ready. I don't believe it."

"Can you talk to her?" Mary asked. "It might come better from you than from a stranger such as myself."

"I think it would come better from someone she'll never

meet again than from a neighbor she'll have to see for years to come."

"That may be the case," Mary admitted. "Where can I find her alone?"

"Victor should be at his office this morning," Nellie replied. "He takes the eight fifteen train."

"I'll leave as soon as I've set Cook off on her task for the day," Mary said, rising from her chair.

Home alone when Mary arrived, Rose Illingsworth was immediately uncooperative. "Rose," Mary argued. "I'm only trying to help."

"Help who, me?"

"Everyone," Mary replied. "The truth will set so many things to rest."

Rose scoffed. "Including the murderer, who'll be hanged."

"Surely that's better than them being free to kill again?" Mary suggested.

"Oh, come in," Rose said, stepping away from the door. "I don't want the neighbors gossiping."

Mary hurried inside.

"You asked if Cyril was with me that day." Rose showed Mary to a chair. "He wasn't."

"Any ideas? He left his house well before nine and turned up at the Marmalades' party right at ten o'clock."

"Victor and I were both here," Rose began. "So you can get what you're thinking out of your mind. Cyril and I did meet with each other, it's true, but not that morning."

"Have you any idea?" Mary persisted, sensing Rose was determined not to venture an opinion.

Rose put her hand to her mouth, as though to hold back her words. Mary waited.

"I sometimes felt," Rose said hesitantly, "there was someone else."

"Was it just a feeling?"

Again, Rose struggled to speak. "There were sometimes marks on his body. He said they were from gardening, or some other excuse, but he wasn't convincing. I think he let me see them just so I'd know I wasn't the only one. It sounds strange, but that's what I thought."

"Is that something he would do?"

"He liked excitement in his lovemaking," Rose said. "More than once, he dawdled getting dressed so he'd be leaving out the back door as Victor was coming in the front. It frightened me, and he liked that too."

"But you don't know who?"

"There aren't many women of our age in the village who are our, well, our class of person, and Cyril was an awful snob."

"You suspected it was Nellie?"

Rose bobbed her head.

"But you have no actual evidence of that?"

"Which is why I'm reluctant even to suggest it," Rose said. "But I don't know who else it could be."

Mary considered this carefully. *Nellie had been at the house to greet the guests when they arrived for the tennis tournament, but could she have only just arrived? Mary didn't remember her looking like someone newly out of a lover's bed. And Gerry arrived after the guests, so he wouldn't have known if his wife had been home or not that morning. Oh no!*

"Can you remember any times when Cyril was supposed to be with you and wasn't? When Nellie might have been out of sight too?"

Rose shook her head. "Cyril was always punctual. He had a tremendous appetite for life."

"Sadly for my investigation," Mary said, smiling, "he appears to have had too much appetite for everything."

"It's true," Rose said. "He ate and drank to excess; he played every game as if it were a final event in the Olympics; he smoked cigars like cheap cigarettes; he attacked everything he did with a passion you wouldn't believe in a man of his age. Incredible energy and stamina . . ." She stopped, her face blushing red.

"That must've been exciting," Mary replied, though it sounded wearisome to her. *All that's behind me, thank heaven.*

"You won't tell Nellie what I thought, will you?"

Mary shook her head. "No, I won't. If you're right, she might be a suspect." The thought of her old friend as the murderer haunted her. If Rose was right, what then? Could she condemn Nellie and Gerry to the gallows?

"Don't tell the police," Rose cried.

"You haven't told them?"

"No and I won't," Rose said. "My suspicions were partly grounded in jealousy, I'm ashamed to say." She paused. "There is something I should mention, but I don't think it has anything to do with Cyril's death."

"What is it?"

"Victor knew something about Gerry and Beacham," Rose said slowly. "He wouldn't tell me what, because he said I'd blab it all over the village."

"About both of them?" Mary prodded.

"Yes. It was something they'd both been involved in. I assumed it would be about local politics, some deal they'd arranged, maybe, and that's too boring for words."

"Did Victor say where he'd learned this?"

Rose wagged her head. "No, it just came out one day when

he was angry about Beacham, but he shut up the moment he saw I was listening."

Mary thanked Rose and reassured her of her complete discretion, then Mary left the house just in time to catch Margie and Dotty in the street. She hailed them, and they met up.

"We should join Winnie in the café," Dotty said. "She'll be wondering where we are."

Winnie was sipping her tea, a plate of crumbs in front of her, when they joined her.

"Have you heard anything juicy?" Dotty whispered after the server had taken the order from the new arrivals.

Winnie's expression was noncommittal. "Have you?"

"We have," Margie whispered, though the café was empty of customers other than themselves. "Mrs. Beacham wasn't at home either that morning."

"What?" Mary asked.

"It's true," Margie replied. "She went out for a walk and only got back in time to change into her tennis dress and leave."

"Where did she walk?" Mary asked, before signaling for silence as the server exited the kitchen with a tray of cups, saucers, and plates for them.

Once the server returned to the kitchen, Dotty said, "Just walking along the lane behind their house. We're going to follow it after our tea to figure out what she might have seen."

"Good thinking," Mary said. "I'll join you."

"And what did you discover, Lady Mary?" Margie asked.

Mary told them Rose had been with her husband, Victor, and left it at that. *If the Illingsworths were together, that leaves Fran and Nellie as the two women who might be suspects and Gerry as the only man. What if Margie learns anything of what I heard?*

Winnie nodded. "That's what we'd heard from the servants."

"The path behind the house sounds promising to me, and yes, we'll follow it after our afternoon tea," Mary said, then silenced them once again as the server came out with their tea and the platter they had ordered of treats to share. *Should I stop investigating before I condemn my friends? Or should I press on in the hope I'll clear their name?*

The footpath that wound its way between the fields and behind the Beachams' was narrow, with tall plants, Queen Anne's Lace mainly, crowding in on it at the start. Farther along, tall hedgerows filled with honeysuckle flowers spilling out from the hawthorns. The sweet honeysuckle scent was intoxicating, and for a time, Mary was so entranced with it she almost forgot why they were there, until Margie woke her by pointing to their left and stating, "There's the Beachams' house."

The Beachams' house looked like a fine old stone building, covered in ivy, but Mary guessed it was more modern because the houses on either side certainly were.

"We've seen nothing to interest a walker until now," Mary said. "So my guess is Mrs. Beacham didn't walk the way we've come but went the way we're headed. Keep your eyes peeled, girls, for anything that might explain her desire to walk out that morning."

"She was hoping to catch her husband, is my guess," Winnie said.

"It could be exactly the opposite," Dotty said, her expression one of deep thought. "I mean, maybe when her husband was with another woman, Mrs. Beacham was with another man."

The group considered this.

"We've never heard anyone suggest this," Margie said. "Wouldn't someone have noticed?"

"Not if it was new," Dotty said. "And maybe not with everyone's eyes on Mr. Beacham's doings."

"We need to keep an open mind," Mary said. "And your idea is a good one, Dotty. And it's one we haven't considered. This may be the time. Either way, whether Mr. or Mrs. Beacham, we're looking for somewhere two people may meet without being seen."

"Like that old shed." Winnie pointed to a tumbledown wooden building in a field to their right.

"It isn't very romantic," Margie said disgustedly.

"I don't think adulterous affairs are romantic," Dotty said. "I think they're just desperate."

Mary laughed. "In many cases, I think you're right, Dotty. And to your point, we should go and investigate that shed no matter how unlikely it looks."

The shed, however, was as dilapidated inside as out, and they returned to the path, brushing their clothes to rid themselves of dust and cobwebs.

"Beacham's clothes were too clean for him to have been in there, but what about that?" Winnie pointed ahead, at a much newer shed.

"It's certainly a better prospect," Mary said. "It probably replaced the one we just visited."

The shed and its lock were both new. Mary had the girls fan out around the building to search for another entrance. There were windows too small and high up for easy access, even by the Winnie, the thinnest and tallest of the three.

"Mr. Beacham was an active man," Margie said, smiling as they all regrouped by the door. "But he'd never get through any of those windows."

"Could he have had a key?" Dotty suggested.

"It depends whose shed this is," Mary said. "If it was his, yes, or if it belonged to someone who let him use it."

"We need to know who owns this building," Margie said. "Some of our café friends will know."

"We should carry on for a few more minutes," Mary said. "If either of the Beachams was meeting someone along this path, it can't have been much farther. Every step to get here is time wasted for..." She paused, wondering how to phrase this. "For canoodling."

The girls laughed. "No one has said 'canoodling' since 1930, Lady Mary," Winnie explained.

Mary smiled. "Perhaps I'm a little out-of-date with my words."

"Out of time, more like," Winnie scoffed.

"Well, you understood what I said, so it can't be so old-fashioned," Mary retorted. "And my point still stands. If we find nothing else in a minute or two, we can assume it was this shed or nothing."

They stopped at a point on the path where the hedges were much lower. There were no other buildings to be seen.

Turning back, Mary said, "You have a new question to ask of your café customer friends. Who owns that building?"

"We'll have the answer to that by lunchtime," Margie replied confidently.

Back at the house, Mary was informed Major Lennox had phoned. She'd called him on the previous day; he wasn't in. And now he'd called back, and she wasn't in. Mary picked up the phone and rang his number.

"Major Lennox?" she asked when the line was picked up.

"Yes," a deep male voice answered. "Is that Lady Mary Culpeper?"

"It is, Major, and as I mentioned in the message I left with your housekeeper, I would like to hear about my good friend Gerry Marmalade's involvement in an investigation in Berlin in 1945."

"There's nothing to tell, really," Lennox replied. "I'm sure Gerry would've explained it as well as I can."

"He feels he was badly treated over the failed investigation..." Mary began.

"Whoa," Lennox said, "just because nothing was proven

doesn't mean it failed. People are still considered innocent until proven guilty in this country."

"You're right, of course," Mary replied. "I chose my words badly because Gerry feels Beacham was guilty and he failed to prove that. That view has colored my own, I'm afraid."

"I know Gerry still holds a grudge against the army and his commanding officer," Lennox replied. "And I understand why. Everyone was sure Beacham was smuggling out looted goods, but Gerry and I and our team did work hard on the investigation. I think you have to consider the possibility that, if we didn't find anything, it was because Beacham was innocent."

"Did you believe he was up to something?"

Lennox laughed. "Every quartermaster in the army was believed to be squirreling away more of the materials than they doled out. It's a feature of institutional life to believe you're being cheated."

"But did you?" Mary persisted.

Lennox paused. "I did, but after the investigation, I came to believe we'd all wronged him."

"Someone has been sending Beacham threatening letters," Mary said, "demanding money, or the old crime will be brought into the light and Beacham shown to be guilty. Did you know about that?"

"How should I? I haven't spoken to the man since 1945. I didn't even know he lived in the same village as Gerry until I read it in the papers."

"What did you make of that?" Mary asked. "Beacham and Gerry living in the same village, I mean."

Again Lennox paused before answering. "I was taken aback, to be honest. It made the old suspicions about Beacham and Gerry being in cahoots seem likely, which was something I'd dismissed as slanderous back in the day."

"It concerns me a little too," Mary admitted. "But I've known

Gerry for decades, and a more honest man I couldn't find anywhere. In fact, I'd say he was too ordinary to be a successful criminal."

Lennox laughed. "He's a real stickler for everything being done the right way and no deviations, if that's what you mean."

"That's exactly what I mean," Mary agreed. "A criminal has to see the opportunity and work out how to make use of it. Gerry couldn't do that, I'm sure."

"How many of us really know what people might do, if a situation arises?" Lennox responded.

"Gerry also received two anonymous letters," Mary said. "You didn't send them either?"

"I did not," Lennox said coldly.

"Any ideas who might have?"

"Your Grace, Gerry and I only send each other a note with our Christmas cards, and it's been that way for ten years at least. I don't know who his friends or enemies are, so, no, I have no idea."

"You see, it has to be someone who knew about Berlin 1945 and knows where he lives now," Mary persisted.

"I understand, but that person isn't me, and I don't know who it could be. Now, if there's nothing else..."

"Can you think of anything that might help?" Mary continued.

"His old batman might know something," Lennox said. "I don't know where he is now, but someone will."

Mary thanked him and hung up the phone, frustrated. She wanted to believe Lennox, but he was one of only two people she knew of who had the right background. Maybe Ponsonby would have more luck with Corporal Foreman, and the girls would get an answer to the ownership of the shed.

When it seemed like the murder was business related, I was excited to have a new case. Now, when the evidence is pointing to

Gerry, the thought of where this might lead frightens me. And even if the evidence points to a personal animosity, it's still Gerry who's the murderer. All these years being friends with Gerry and now I discover I didn't really know him. Like Lennox had suggested, "who knows what any of us might do if the circumstances were right."

THE GIRLS ARRIVED BACK FIRST, very excited. They hustled Mary out of the drawing room where she'd been talking to Nellie, leaving Nellie in an obvious state of anger at being excluded.

"We have information only for Lady Mary's ears," Margie said, with a triumphant expression that only made Nellie look more fierce.

In the hall, Mary said, "What is it I have to know that Nellie can't?"

"The shed belongs to the farmer whose land it's on, Cutler is his name," Margie said. "But people have seen Beacham using it. He must have had a key."

"And he'd keep the key in his pocket presumably," Mary replied. "So the police must know about the shed. Did anyone see them search it?"

"No one mentioned it," Winnie said.

"What if *she* took the key that day?" Dotty suggested.

"Why would he let her?" Mary asked.

"Who knows, but it would explain why the police haven't searched the shed," Margie said.

Mary puzzled over this for a moment. "And why couldn't your mother hear this, Margie?"

"Because we're going to break into the shed tonight, and Mum will try to stop us."

Mary laughed. "That's true. However, I suggest we wait until

Ponsonby is back." Seeing their faces, Mary added, "He has tools for picking locks, which means no damage to the door, the lock or the windows. This way our visit will be unnoticed by the police when we tell them of the shed's significance."

"When will that be?" Winnie said. "The police might learn of the shed at any time. Tonight is our only safe chance."

"If all has gone well in London, he should be back this afternoon," Mary said. "Have you been given any information about the car problems?"

"The punctures are assumed to be because of construction work being done on a cottage just outside the village—nails falling from a construction vehicle bringing materials to the site."

"And the others?"

"Nothing," Dotty said. "But the café customers aren't really interested in cars or their problems, so they aren't the best people to ask."

"Then we need to find people interested in cars and their problems." Mary smiled. "Any teenage boys in the village?"

"Some," Margie replied.

"Not really our sort," Dotty said mischievously. "And we don't want to give them ideas."

"Then I must interview them," Mary said. "Where would I meet them?"

"In the pub bar," Winnie suggested. "A job for Ponsonby."

"Then we await his return for two reasons. He'll be flattered."

PONSONBY ARRIVED WELL AFTER LUNCH, and Mary immediately whisked him away to her room for a private conference. While he did have burgling tools, which he wouldn't say where or who he'd inherited them from, Ponsonby was an extremely honest man and would take persuading that they had enough evidence to warrant breaking into someone else's property. First, however, Mary wanted to know what Foreman knew, which, it turned out, wasn't much.

"Mr. Foreman hasn't seen Mr. Marmalade in some years, my lady, and was surprised I or anyone would want to know about events of a dozen years ago."

"He couldn't provide any clues? Anyone we don't know of?" Mary asked desperately.

"No, my lady. Nor did he know Mr. Beacham was living in the same village as Mr. Marmalade. He wasn't aware Beacham had been killed."

"Major Lennox was much the same," Mary replied ruefully. "A dead end."

"In the case of Mr. Foreman, I'm sure it is."

"Well, here's what we learned today." Mary told the tale in a way she hoped would make Ponsonby eager to see what was inside the shed.

When she finished, Ponsonby looked very grave. She suspected he might be on the cusp of saying no, and she didn't want that.

"I know this might be against your principles," Mary said quickly, to forestall a refusal, "but if you could teach me how to use those picklocks of yours, I could be in and out of the shed without you being involved at all."

Ponsonby continued thinking, and Mary's heart was sinking when he finally said, "It's wrong, but if we learn where he was, we may learn where he was poisoned, and justice will come from our actions. I'll accompany you, my lady, and open the door."

"Thank you," Mary said. "Your agreement means a lot to me. The girls will want to come too."

"My lady!" Ponsonby's horror was instant. "We shouldn't involve the young people in criminal acts. If we were to be caught, it would blight their lives forever."

Mary grimaced. "I know, but there's no way of stopping them. They're going with or without us, and they'll be much safer if we lead them rather than have them act alone."

Ponsonby shook his head in dismay. "They must act as our lookouts and get away if they see anyone coming. We can't let them become criminals at their age."

"I'll steer them to that," Mary promised. "Now, have something to eat, rest from your journey and be ready to leave at nine o'clock. It will be almost dark by then."

Inspector Acton had come to the manor with Gerry upon his release that evening. When Gerry's return was announced, Acton was met by an angry group of Marmalade family and friends. After Nellie's indignation at the way her husband had been treated died down, the family took Gerry inside and the house was again quiet. All but Mary. She slipped back out into the evening. She set off quickly down the drive with Barkley tugging at the leash.

Acton was standing by his car when she reached him. "What is it?" he asked tersely. It was late, and he clearly wanted to go home.

"What did you discover about Gerry Marmalade?"

"Not a lot."

"But you let him go," Mary said.

"Only because we haven't yet got enough to arrest him," Acton said. "Your information will, I think, be crucial in bringing him to justice."

His words sent a shiver down her spine. Her role would come out, and she'd lose her friends, right or wrong.

"I was hoping to hear you'd cleared him," Mary said sadly.

"I understand your concern," he said seriously. "But I fear he may well be guilty. You should prepare yourself for that."

Mary thanked him and set off to allow Barkley his chance to chase rabbits. She'd always had to restrain him, and the tug-of-war exercise was good for both of them. She had only an hour or so before she and the rest of the sleuths went house-, or shed-, breaking.

The police haven't mentioned Nellie—why not? Are they unaware of her possible motives? Should she point them to look at Nellie? She'd done that with Gerry, and the police had decided he was likely guilty of something. *What if I'm wrong about this? And I dearly hope I am.* The evidence was thin, and the police may think she was acting out of personal spite. *What to do?*

14

UNSEEN BACKHAND

The summer evening sky was still light enough a half hour past sunset for Mary and her gaggle of assistants to make their way along the path to the shed. Lights were on in the houses they passed, but with the trees and hedgerows shrouding their passage, they felt themselves safe from prying eyes.

When she raised the issue, the girls had resisted Mary's instructions for them to act as lookouts and not enter the shed, but eventually, after stressing the possibility of a lifetime criminal record, Mary persuaded them it was best.

At the gate in the hedge that led to the shed, Mary instructed her lookouts how to make a wide circle around the building.

"Remember," she reminded them, "you warn us with an owl hoot, and then you leave quickly before you're seen or caught."

Silently, the group dispersed through the gate and along the lane to their designated observation posts. Mary and Ponsonby hurried to the door, and Ponsonby began opening the lock.

He jiggled his tool for less than a minute, then removed the padlock and tugged at the door. It opened silently, its hinges well oiled.

Inside, they switched on their flashlights and scanned the

interior. At first sight, it was mainly a storage area, but a flight of wooden steps led up to a second story.

Ponsonby crept forward and slowly climbed the steps. At the top, he swept his torch around. "Someone uses this for a place to sleep, my lady."

Mary followed, and they both knelt on the floor, the sloping roof too low for standing. A fine, thick mattress and neatly folded sheets on a low bed frame made up the principal furniture. It was hidden from the ground floor by a low chest of drawers with ropes piled on top. The bed had a headboard butting against, and fastened to, the wall of the shed. It was a substantial piece of furniture, made of a hardwood, maybe mahogany. It was hard to tell in the gloom. An expensive piece of Victorian furnishing. Beacham must have picked it up at an estate sale.

They shuffled nearer to the bed and drawers, pleasantly surprised to find the carpet on the floor sufficiently thick to protect their mature knees. A hint of cigar smoke lingering in the air and Mary slipped on a glove before sliding open the first of three drawers in the credenza. It was filled with clothes—women's clothes, but of a particularly erotic kind. *Victorian music-hall showgirl. Scandalous!*

Ponsonby examined under the edges of the mattress and around the intricately carved headboard. "I think Mr. Beacham liked playing the games found in lurid low-quality novels, my lady. There are abrasions in the swirls of the headboard that suggest ropes were tied here."

"The clothes here have the same feel about them." Mary opened another drawer. "And these items suggest playful punishment."

"Do any of them suggest who wore them?" Ponsonby asked. "Nothing I've found says who came here. They cleaned up well after themselves."

"Not yet." Mary pushed aside the assorted items in the drawer before closing it and opening another. "The police might get fingerprints from the handles of these things, but my bet is on the prints being Beacham's."

"But that means one of his lovers must have gone home marked, and surely her husband would notice?" Ponsonby said.

Mary frowned. "You're right. I was too conventional in my thinking. And Fran would notice if *he* came home marked."

"Maybe Beacham and his wife were no longer sharing a bed."

"The same might be said for our mystery mistress," Mary argued. "We can hardly ask them, can we?"

"No, my lady, though perhaps you might get a hint if you spoke to them." Mary lifted a crook-handled schoolmaster's cane from the next drawer she opened. "Mr. Beacham remembering his school days, do you think?"

"It seems so," Mary replied. "Or imagining himself in the role of schoolmaster, perhaps." She paused, then chuckled.

"The image is quite ridiculous, I agree." Ponsonby almost smiled.

"I just thought," Mary said, "that morning Beacham was whacking a tennis ball back and forth, and here we find he has a penchant for another kind of whacking. Mrs. Illingsworth said he had a great appetite for life and embraced everything with gusto, including his lovemaking."

"Do you think this is what she meant?" Ponsonby asked.

Mary paused. "She said he liked to frighten her by delaying his departure when he knew her husband was about to come home. She didn't mention anything like this."

"There are many ways of inducing fright, my lady."

Mary nodded. "Now, what do we tell the girls?"

"As little as possible," Ponsonby said. "This is a place for lovers to meet, but no evidence it was Beacham or any of his lovers who met here."

"We must be sure of that," Mary said. "I'll continue with the drawers. You continue around the bed and the corners of the room. Something might have been missed in a corner somewhere."

Their search, however, found nothing to link Beacham or any of the women in the village to this loft space.

"The lovers here were extremely careful," Mary said, when they'd finally given up and were making their way down.

"I agree, my lady," Ponsonby said. "If I didn't know it was impossible, I'd say they had a member of their household staff clean up after."

Which might explain why he didn't have the key in his pockets. "We can't stay much longer," Mary said, nodding. "But we should look down here as well. Particularly below the loft. Something may have fallen from the upper story. We might find it."

Empty-handed here as well. It's so frustrating. Are we getting any closer to the truth? I feel we're still far removed from it.

They exited the shed and locked the padlock back onto the door.

Giving the agreed signal, the low hoot of an owl, brought the girls in from their stations. They were full of questions and bitterly disappointed at the answers.

"Are you sure you looked everywhere?" Margie complained. "Can't we go and search?"

"We looked everywhere." Mary led them out through the field gate onto the small path, which was now so dark, they needed their flashlights to walk safely.

"How can people in a mad passion not leave something behind?" Winnie demanded.

"It proves my point," Dotty said. "Not a mad passion at all. Just desperation."

"Oh, shut up, Dotty," Margie said. "Just because the boy you liked didn't dance with you the other night doesn't mean everyone's love life is sad."

"Girls," Mary said. "This conversation would be best kept to yourselves. And we have to pass the houses up ahead without being seen or heard."

PONSONBY RETURNED from the village pub close to midnight, with his report on what the young men of the village knew about cars. "They confirmed the likelihood of the puncture being due to the cowboy builders working on the edge of the village. As for the Illingsworth car's brake failure, their suggestion was Victor didn't service his car with reputable dealers. He used old Fred Cobbly in the village, who was blind, deaf, and forgetful. Fred probably forgot to tighten the joints and didn't see the fluid dripping as Victor drove away. The other car failure was probably, in the mind of these young experts, because these villagers drove cars that were old crocks from the '40s, wartime relics for the most part."

"I hope you put them right on this last point, Ponsonby," Mary said, aggrieved by a description of the village cars that also fit her own. "Our Rolls is as good as the day it was made."

Ponsonby replied gravely, "The supply of information would dry up if I start challenging their uneducated assumptions."

"Did they say that?" Mary asked.

"The phrase used was 'You just want to protect your friends. Why should we help you do that?'"

"Hmm," Mary said. "I'd like to give them a piece of my mind."

Ponsonby changed the subject. "You mentioned earlier about Mr. Beacham whacking tennis balls and then whacking with the cane, or being whacked, of course, but it occurs to me there's yet another instance of this word to consider. I believe in gangster films the word is used to denote being killed."

Mary smiled. It wasn't often Ponsonby offered a humorous insight into events. "I believe you're right. And he was royally whacked in this instance; he couldn't get more whacked. Still, while I see the odd coincidence of the words, I can't believe it's a clue."

"I'm sure it isn't." Ponsonby nodded. "But the strangeness of it amused me. Good night, my lady."

As Mary prepared for bed, she pondered the suspects, trying to find something that suggested one over the other. Rose said she had an alibi in her husband, but it was equally true her husband, Victor, had an alibi in Rose. Neither could be ruled out, though the love nest had a strong hint of the female about it—and not just the clothes, which were much too small for either Victor or Cyril. There was also, as Ponsonby had noticed, a tidiness that suggested a woman's hand.

Rose had suspected Nellie, and while Nellie could be the mystery mistress of the loft, she couldn't have poisoned Cyril that morning, for she was definitely at home preparing for the tennis party. Her maid had confirmed that. Gerry may have poisoned Beacham in some way that morning, but he wasn't ever in that love nest, Mary was sure of that. The scent of cigars lingered there, but not pipe-smoke, and Gerry always had a pipe going.

Fran Beacham had been out and about, possibly spying on her husband. *But if he'd been in the loft, his lover would've been there too, and Cyril was the only victim. Maybe, of course, same as if it was Gerry, Fran could have found another way to poison her husband—breakfast maybe? I'll ask Inspector Acton when next he appears.*

As these speculations played in her head, another possibility leapt in. *What was the real reason Margie didn't want to interview the young men of the village?* It was all very unsatisfactory, she decided, and switched off the light.

15

NETTING THE TRUTH

Mary woke the following morning from a restless sleep, where she'd dreamt of Margie holding a dripping syringe. Once fully awake, she prepared herself for the day and reminded herself Margie couldn't have killed Beacham—she'd been with Dotty and Winnie that morning. Mary herself could vouch for that.

She stepped to her open window as Acton pulled around the drive. By the time she arrived downstairs, the Marmalade family, Dotty and Winnie had already greeted him, but Mary asserted herself to be the first to question the inspector.

"Is the rest of the postmortem report finished, Inspector?"

"Yes."

Used to the police avoiding sharing information, Mary continued, "And do we know now how the poison was administered?"

"We do," Acton replied.

"Inspector, the staff of three households are under considerable stress because of the suspicion the poison might be in the food they prepared that day," Mary said. "Even if you have no concern for our feelings, you might think of theirs."

Acton flashed a considerate expression. "You can set their minds at rest. The poison was not in the food he ate, nor his drinks. In fact he ate an unusual breakfast, none of which was on the menus we had described to us."

"So he ate somewhere other than here or at his home?" Nellie beamed with relief.

"That's correct, madam," Acton said, though the twitch in his jaw revealed to Mary that he was holding onto information, and she wanted to know what it was. "You may reassure your staff they aren't under any suspicion in that regard."

"Are they under suspicion in other regards?" Mary asked and Acton shook his head.

"What he ate masked the strong sedative he was given," Acton said.

"Was he killed by a sedative?" Mary asked, puzzled.

"No. He was then injected with a high dose of nicotine commonly found in pest control products. It was slow to act, so he died far away from where this all happened, as the murderer had planned."

"The cat and the dog again," Mary said to Acton.

"Apparently so. We exhumed the dog and confirmed it was the same nicotine fluid used on the victim."

"You have been busy," Mary replied. "Does the doctor say how long between the injection and time of death?"

"He thinks about three hours, but Mr. Beacham's indulgence of cigars and his exertions on the tennis court may have brought on an earlier death."

Mary considered. *Then the injection happened around seven or eight thirty that morning, or perhaps even a little later. Did anyone see Beacham at that time? What time did Fran walk that morning? What about dog walkers? That path was clearly used by them.* She needed the girls back out, questioning everyone, and quietly told them to meet with her when Acton was gone and Nellie and

Gerry had withdrawn for some private moments; it would take time for everyone to come to terms with what had happened.

"You won't be telling everyone what you told us, will you?" Mary asked.

"I won't," Acton replied. "You may tell your staff and the staff who helped here that morning they aren't suspected, but I'd like you to keep most of this to yourselves. I only explained because I know Mr. Marmalade"—he gestured at Gerry, whose silence remained thunderous—"will have gleaned much of it from our questioning."

"You said 'masked,' Inspector," Mary said. "Can you tell us more about that?"

"Not at this time," Acton said. "Unfortunately, the ingredients are fairly common in well-to-do households, but we still hope our searches will tell us where the food was prepared."

"Surely, the murderer will have cleared away all traces by now?" Nellie said.

"Undoubtedly," Acton said. "And yet we remain hopeful. Which brings me to the next thing I came to say. We intend to go through the rubbish bins of every house in the village."

"Of course. Bin day is every other Thursday," Nellie said. "You think a tin or a bottle will be in one of them?"

Acton shrugged. "It's possible, though it's also possible the murderer realized that too, and disposed of the evidence some other way. We have to check."

"You can start with ours, Inspector," Nellie said, "as you're here."

Acton grinned. "Thank you, Mrs. Marmalade, but my men are already doing that."

"Shouldn't you have been given permission first, or are you considering garbage public property, where you wouldn't need permission?"

"I assume any honest person would have no objection,"

Acton said. "Anyone can go through those bins, not just the police. If there are no other questions or comments, I'll be on my way." Everyone was quiet, so Acton left the room. He crossed the terrace, heading for the side of the house where the bins were kept.

"I wish he had to go through them all himself," Nellie snapped. "It would serve him right."

"What might be in cans or jars," Margie asked, "that would be unusual enough to look for, but not out of the ordinary in houses such as ours?"

Everyone stared blankly at her for a moment, then Dotty said, "Artichoke hearts."

"Olives," Winnie added.

"Good suggestions, girls," Mary said. "But I'm not sure they're highly flavored enough or unusual for breakfast items."

"But that's the point," Margie said. "Unusual, but not unlikely. We had olives for breakfast when we visited the south of France last year."

"I wonder if he meant kedgeree?" Nellie asked. "It's old-fashioned, I know, but I've had it for breakfast many times."

"Or deviled kidneys," Winnie said. "Not my cup of tea, but they're often on a breakfast buffet when we're guests at friends' houses."

"There are many possible items," Mary agreed. "But kidneys and smoked fish aren't usually bought in cans or jars."

"But we don't know they're looking for tins or jars," Dotty said. "There are other kinds of wrappers they might find in a bin."

"Maybe we should ask the village shopkeepers if they've sold any of those items lately," Nellie said thoughtfully.

"If we could discover what the items were," Mary agreed. "But it would raise suspicion if I went to the butcher and fishmonger with a long list."

"Not us," Margie said, with a sly grin. "They won't be suspicious of young people who've never shopped for groceries asking questions about ingredients."

"Very well. But we'll make the list of possible items and find out what else similar has been bought recently," Mary said. "Now, who has the best relationship with Constable Watkins and/or Sergeant Reynolds?"

"I know both Watkins and Reynolds quite well," Gerry said, suddenly breaking his long silence. "And after the last two days, they owe me a favor."

"Can you discover from them what Acton was so cagey about telling us?" Mary asked.

"I can try, but we'd best leave it until later today, when a long enough period of time has passed for the three of us to talk as old friends and neighbors."

"Anything more for us, Lady Mary?" Margie asked.

"I do have one more job for you, yes, but we'll talk about that as we take Barkley for a walk. He'll explode if he doesn't get outside soon."

With Barkley scampering beside them, Lady Mary and her assistants strolled into the village.

"Tell us, Lady Mary," Winnie drawled. "Are we finally getting somewhere?"

"Well, we now know how he died. First a strong sedative and then the lethal injection of a slow-acting poison. We need to know who uses sedatives..."

"Half the women in the country use sleeping pills, Lady Mary. Don't you listen to the news?" Dotty asked.

Mary smiled. "I do, and I don't believe half of it."

"Which half?" Winnie grinned mischievously.

"Both halves," Mary said. "I've been involved in many things reported in the news in my lifetime, and practically nothing of what they said was true. If they can't be honest in little things, I certainly wouldn't believe them in big things."

"So we have to ask who takes sleeping pills?" Margie asked.

"Yes, but only as we follow the threads we have to the end."

"Such as?" Winnie asked.

Mary smiled. "Here's what I want. The people in the houses that back onto the path that leads to the shed will have seen walkers along there day after day. Who did they see? We need a list. I suspect many will be dog walkers and can be left until later, but anyone who walks along there alone could be our mystery mistress."

"Oh," Winnie said. "I like the sound of a 'mystery mistress.' I could imagine myself in that role."

"Winnie!" Margie and Dotty cried out.

"Just for acting," Winnie replied. "I'd love to be a femme fatale in a movie. Though, to be honest, I'd prefer a more sophisticated place than a farmer's shed."

Mary laughed. "Well, even femme fatales must start somewhere, I guess."

Winnie shook her head. "They start at the top, otherwise what's the point?"

When they reached the village green, the discussion had degenerated into the relative merits of the screen's many femme fatales and the unlikelihood of Winnie emulating any of them. Mary reminded them of their task and left them bickering.

They're still young, they'll learn. Sadly, we all do.

Mary walked back through the village and headed straight to Fran Beacham's house. She rang the bell, and a maid answered the door expediently. Mary introduced herself, but the woman said, "Mrs. Beacham is out at present, Your Ladyship. I'll tell her you called."

"Thank you." Mary turned to leave, then paused. "Has Mrs. Beacham gone for a walk along the path behind her house?"

"Why, yes, she often does."

Barkley barked excitedly, as if he knew they had a new task. *Hunt down Fran Beacham.* He sniffed at the doorstep and path for a scent to follow.

Mary smiled. "It's a wonderful path. I walked that way just yesterday, and the scent of honeysuckle almost made me giddy. And the views across the valley when you get past the hedge are wonderful."

"It is magnificent," the maid replied, with more enthusiasm than would be expected from someone who sees the sight every day.

"May I cut through the garden and follow the path from here? I'll likely meet Mrs. Beacham returning from her walk."

"Certainly, Your Ladyship, come through the house." She stepped aside, and Mary and Barkley followed her through to a set of French windows that opened onto a terrace with steps down to the lawn.

The gate out to the path was overhung by a wooden arch supporting a clematis, whose flowers were almost past their bloom. *I wish I could've seen them earlier in the season.* Barkley ignored the clematis—no scent—and picked up the scent he'd found at the front doorstep. He finally had something worthwhile to do.

Unlatching and opening the gate, Mary entered the path she'd followed the day before. Barkley stuck close to Mary's side at first. Again, the heady scent of the honeysuckle was overpowering, as if it could lull the walker into sleep and transport them to a magical alternative world. *This isn't, but could be, Narnia.*

Honeysuckle didn't mask the scent Barkley was following. He ignored it and rushed ahead of her.

Mary quickened her pace in pursuit of Fran Beacham, and now, she smiled, watching her canine sleuth, Barkley, hard at work. Soon Barkley realized she wasn't close behind, and he had to stop, his rectangular form was like a loaf of bread as he patiently waited for Mary.

They'd made good time, having gone well beyond the shed before Mary finally stopped. Nestled down in the valley, about a mile away, lay an old but well-kept farm. *Is this where Fran went? Or was she in the shed with its surprising love nest? Or one of the houses farther along the lane?*

Though Barkley was raring to go to the farm, Mary had no wish to walk the mile to and from on such a warm day—*nor do I want to approach the Beachams' neighbors in such a way.*

"Let's turn back, Barkley. Maybe we'll catch Fran back in the village." She directed Barkley to follow her and began walking toward the village.

She retraced her steps to the shed. *Locked, so that removes one possibility.*

"What about the neighboring houses or the farm?" she said absentmindedly, and Barkley barked his approval. "Of course you want to go to the farm." She chuckled. *I can hardly knock on their doors and ask for Fran.* It was possible Fran had come out to the path but turned the other way and went *into* the village. *She could be sipping tea with Rose Illingsworth. Now that's a tête-à-tête I would pay money to see.*

Barkley woofed again as if he wanted to catch her attention. He trotted back and forth, sniffing the ground but staying close to Mary. Everyone who knew her also knew she loved her dog dearly, that they seemed to have their own way to communicate with each other. But here, now, she cogitated about what would be the obvious clues before her if she had the keen senses of her dog. She giggled at the thought.

Mary could understand the many reasons Fran would go out walking on nice summer's days. Possibly a lover here somewhere —*everyone else is doing it.* It could just be to calm her spirit after the death of her husband, if she still had feelings for him. It could be to enjoy one of England's rare warm days of sunshine. With autumn and winter coming on, it wouldn't be unlikely. It would be a long winter alone in the house.

"Just because Cyril was a philanderer," Mary muttered to herself, "you shouldn't assume his wife was too." And yet, it had been suggested the aggrieved wife, Rose, had taken lovers out of a wish for revenge. The police had let Gerry go after a full day of questioning, but what about Fran? If Gerry was out of the house that morning, and didn't return until just after their guests had arrived, could Nellie have been away too? *The staff say she was home, but they were in the kitchen preparing food.* Could Nellie be the murderer?

Mary was uncomfortable whenever this train of thinking popped into her head. *I told the girls they must be clear-sighted in gathering and assessing the evidence, but on this question, I'm not. I must ask the staff to once again confirm Nellie was in the house that morning.*

16

VOLLEY OF ACCUSATIONS

The village was quiet, and after peeking into several shops, Mary spied her young sleuths diligently asking questions. For the moment, Mary gave up searching for Fran Beacham. If there was any truth in her suspicions, surely Nellie would've uncovered something about it. People being in unusual places or with odd people always gave rise to the gossip of watchful villagers. But would Nellie tell her if she was the one involved?

Nellie had claimed she'd discovered nothing linking Fran Beacham to anyone, and Mary was left perplexed. *Where was Fran that morning?* Now Mary was doubting Nellie. *Where is she, and how does she fit into the puzzle? Maybe they were both together? One administered the sedative and one the poison? Don't get ahead of yourself, Mary, now you're just frustrated and jumping to conclusions!*

"Sister sleuths," Mary said as the girls left, "what have you learned so far?"

"Nothing yet," Margie said despondently.

"That's disappointing," Mary replied. "I'd been hoping to find Fran in the village. Have you seen her?"

The three girls shook their heads.

"Pother!" Mary said dramatically. "She's out and about somewhere."

"She could be visiting my mum," Margie suggested.

Mary nodded. "You may be right. I'll return to the house. If nothing else, I can chew the cud with Ponsonby on this frustrating case."

FRAN WAS NOT WITH NELLIE. Mary could see Nellie was alone, sitting in her favorite chair by the window, leaving Mary to follow her alternate line of inquiry. Joining Ponsonby in the garden, where he was watching the gardener remove summer annuals and plant autumn ones, she suggested they walk.

When they were well away from the gardener, Mary spoke, "On the nights you've visited, has there been any gossip in the pub about Fran and Cyril?" Barkley trotted between them, always happy to be following a trail.

Ponsonby's expression was frigid. "We do not talk about such things in the men's side of the pub."

He's never this outraged. "Maybe I should try the ladies lounge, they might be more forthcoming."

"I can't think ladies would talk about such matters in a public place either."

"You may be right, and I doubt they'd tell me if I joined them," Mary replied. "And maybe I'm making too much of her being out along that path on two occasions, one of which was when Beacham was being injected with insect poison."

"My lady, I fear many people go out for a stroll in the country. It may have no significance whatsoever."

"Then why couldn't I find her today? The path is narrow and runs between fields. She wasn't sitting in the meadows, and she wasn't to be seen anywhere along the path," Mary muttered. "Surely, Barkley would've sniffed her out if she was out of my sightline."

The indignant corgi growled.

"True. I suggest the girls may have more success asking among the young people about Mrs. Beacham's solitary walks, if there's gossip to be shared—"

"Good. That can be their task after they've found out who walks along the path often." And as luck would have it, there were the girls just as the trail led Mary, Barkley and Ponsonby back toward the house.

Her assistants were brimming over with excitement and energy. So much that Barkley became overloaded, his ears not able to keep up with the tittering.

Dotty beamed. "I have a new suspect." She swept her eyes around the group in triumph. "The fishmonger. He sold mainly cod, haddock, sole and salmon over the past week, but he did sell some smoked haddock to General Lowther's cook only a few days ago, before the murder for sure."

"That's for kedgeree," Margie said. "And it isn't a strong clue. General Lowther was with the Indian Army for years before India's independence. He loves all the foods of the old Anglo-Indian menu."

"He could have visited the General anytime these past years. And it was Beacham at the love nest, not Lowther."

Margie frowned. "You know, Dotty has a point. I remember dad saying that Beacham had sold some Indian relics for General Lowther, and Lowther was dismayed, having been badly advised. He saw the same relic in a London shop for much more than Beacham had given him."

"Before we go wild on this new lead," Mary said, "Margie, tell us what you learned."

"I interviewed our butcher, well, his son anyway, and as well as the usual cuts of beef, lamb, bacon and pork, they sold kidneys to our cook and to the Illingsworths'."

"Those deviled kidneys," Margie said, smiling. "But, just so you know, ours went into a steak and kidney pudding."

"But not necessarily all of them," Mary mused. "Still, we must continue. Winnie, what do you have?"

Having waited stoically for her turn to talk, Winnie relayed, "I spoke to the greengrocer, and, of the kinds of things we're looking for, they sold olives, pimentos, sardines, pilchards, mussels, oysters and, would you believe it, tiny frankfurter sausages in a can."

"I've had them," Dotty said. "They're tasty, and quite strong-tasting."

"Saying sausage reminds me," Margie said, "the butcher mentioned smoky bacon. Apparently it isn't a big seller around here, but they keep some in for Mr. Beacham."

"Now that might be a clue also," Mary said. "If someone fed Beacham a sedative, it might well be in his favorite smoky bacon."

"All the things on the greengrocer's list are clues," Winnie said, exasperated. "And most are breakfast items."

"Such as?" Dotty asked, unconvinced.

"Olives, pilchards or sardines on toast, frankfurters chopped and wrapped in bacon, or oysters wrapped in bacon, *angels on horseback*," Winnie said. "We've had them at home for breakfast. Papa says they're too good for just hors d'oeuvres."

"All good information, ladies, and thank you for gathering this," Mary said, as once again the discussion was getting out of hand. "But interviewing shopkeepers wasn't what you set out to do."

Margie replied, airily, "We did both together. It seemed easiest, and everyone knows we're investigating anyway."

Mary nodded. "And did you learn anything from people who may have used the trail?"

"Not really," Winnie replied. "No one is ready to say they were up and about that morning. No one knows anything," she finished, disgustedly.

"There must be dog walkers," Mary mused. "We need to find a dog walker."

"They may all use different paths," Dotty said, her brow furrowed in thought. "The path we're interested in doesn't give a lot of scope for a dog. It's too narrow and confined."

"Well," Mary said, "your information from the shopkeepers does give some possible leads, but until we know what Beacham ate that morning, they're just guesses."

"It's also not a foolproof result," Nellie said, frowning. "The police have it right. Packaging may be in the bins right now, but it doesn't prove the items were bought in the last week. Tinned or bottled goods could have been bought weeks ago."

"True," said Mary. "But this may have been a last-minute decision—to kill Mr. Beacham, I mean—and it's possible the means to do it wasn't at hand and had to be bought. We need to log our findings for further review when we know more."

"I think," Winnie said, "what this new information confirms is that the murderer is a woman. After all, you can't imagine a man providing him with his favorite breakfast. No man would even know he *had* a favorite breakfast."

"Are you sure?" Margie asked. "Why wouldn't a man know that?"

Winnie laughed. "Ask your father what your, or your mother's, favorite breakfast is and then ask your mum what your father's is. Or ask yourself."

"Papa always has bacon, egg, mushrooms, and fried bread," Margie said.

"Now ask your parents," Winnie replied.

"I suspect Winnie is right," Mary said. "Men never care about things like that. We suspected it could've been a woman, but this does suggest it really is."

"Which," Dotty said slowly, "explains why the authorities didn't see the injection mark right away." She flushed red, before continuing, "The injection was probably somewhere very private."

The listening group was silent for a moment. Dotty's words had been delivered in such a serious tone, immediate contradictions or even agreement would be frivolous.

Finally, Mary replied, "It's true. This crime needed planning and a good understanding of what would deliver Beacham into her power long enough to inject him. She had to get the sedative, a hypodermic, and the insect poison, as well as the mysterious foodstuffs and have them all on hand that day."

"A lot of people take sleeping pills," Margie said. "And if she was his lover, she already knew a lot about what would make this possible. Even a hypodermic isn't so hard to find these days, and the insect poison was in more than one local garden shed."

"Well, the only thing wrong with this picture is why a female lover would want to kill him." Mary said.

Margie raised her eyebrows and flashed a 'that's obvious' expression at Mary.

Mary continued, "but, we have a good summing up of what we know and what we suspect. Now we just have to identify the woman."

"There are only two possible suspects, in my mind," Margie added. "Fran Beacham and Rose Illingsworth. Cyril liked his ladies to be mature."

Mary remembered Rose Illingsworth's suspicions and said nothing. Nellie was still very much in her mind because, while

Nellie may have been working on the tournament preparations between nine and ten o'clock, Beacham was injected at around seven thirty.

Margie's expression was one of a wish to speak but without yet having decided how to say it.

"Yes, Margie?" Mary prompted.

"I did hear, from people in the village, that he didn't always go for mature women," she said at last. "There were rumors about flings with younger women."

"Do you know names?" Mary asked.

Margie shook her head, her face flushed.

"We've definitely ruled out Victor Illingsworth, then?" Winnie asked, when it became clear Margie wasn't about to add more.

"Or General Lowther," Dotty added.

"Not definitely," Mary said, thinking carefully as she spoke. "General Lowther would very likely have unusual food for breakfast and may well have had the means to do the rest. Older people use sleeping pills and often have injections, if he was diabetic for example. No, I think he must be investigated."

Dotty beamed with pleasure. "I'll do that. I'm sure he's the killer. I think all this love nest and womanizing is just getting in the way of us seeing it's a very simple crime of revenge."

"Fran, Rose, and General Lowther, then?" Winnie asked again.

"We must confirm where Fran Beacham and Rose Illingsworth were that morning." Mary nodded. "While Dotty gets the background on General Lowther and Ponsonby finds out more about Beacham's partner."

"I can start Dotty off on that," Margie said. "We know him quite well."

With that agreed, the group broke up to begin their new

assignments. Mary, Ponsonby, and Cook then met in Mary's room to decide on their roles.

"If any of what we've learned is true," Ponsonby began, "we can rule out Beacham's business partner."

"We can't rule him out. He could've been here," Mary replied. "Maybe he brought a treat from London for a breakfast meeting. But why would they do this in secret?"

"Maybe," Cook said grimly, "they weren't just partners in business. You hear about that sort of thing in London."

Mary smiled at Cook's country prejudice against city folk. "We should consider this angle without involving the girls. Your job, Ponsonby, I think."

"I'll catch the next train, my lady," Ponsonby replied. "Maybe his neighbors and fellow gallery owners could shed some light on his location that morning."

"I'll go back to the cooks, milady," Cook said. "They'll know who likes their breakfasts flavorful. I don't hold with that kind of thing myself—simple porridge is good enough for anyone's breakfast."

"Do you have Scot in your blood, Cook?" Mary laughed.

"Aye, I do, and Norfolk as well. Maybe we're simple folk, but ruining your stomach with fancy spices first thing in the morning isn't sensible, whatever your station in life." With this parting shot, Cook left to begin questioning the village families' cooks all over again.

Mary smiled as the door closed firmly behind as Cook departed. "I fear we shall be persona non grata with the village servants should we ever come again," she said to Ponsonby.

"If we solve the murder, my lady, we'll be welcomed everywhere in Upper Wainbury. There's a lot of concern about this case."

"Phone me tonight," Mary said. "Even if you haven't learned anything."

"Very well, my lady. I'll be packed and ready for the next train."

Barkley buzzed with energy, his ears quivering at Mary's every word.

"I'll take Barkley for a walk to General Lowther's house," Mary commented, staring at the busy dog. "Burn off some of his high spirits, and if I'm lucky, the general may be in his garden, and we can enjoy a *neighborly* chat."

As she left the house, Inspector Acton was getting into his car to leave. She crossed the graveled drive to greet him, and he stepped out of his car.

"Good evening, Inspector," Mary said brightly.

"Evening," Acton replied.

"Can we talk about Gerry?"

"Depends what you mean by 'talk'?" Acton lifted his briefcase from the car.

"Have you learned enough to clear him?"

Acton considered his reply. "London has talked to many of Mr. Marmalade's fellow officers, and while the jury is still out in my mind, there's no evidence he's the murderer."

"So, I should forget about Gerry as a suspect?"

"I think you should forget about any suspects." Acton grinned. "I assume you won't, and therefore I think you were wrong about Mr. Marmalade."

Mary frowned. His advice was a relief and a concern, but had they done a real investigation? It was very quick. Were the accomplices back in 1945 now in prominent positions and able to shut today's investigation down? How likely was that?

"Thank you, Inspector," she said at last. "I'll look elsewhere for a solution." She bent and patted Barkley, who'd settled into a snooze on her toes, and they left the inspector so he could get back on his way.

Unfortunately, if it wasn't Gerry or Fran, the most likely

suspect was Nellie. That was even more frightening than it being Gerry and tied to an event thirteen years ago. She must interview the Marmalades' cook and maid herself, but how? Nellie would soon learn of her questioning the staff and be rightly outraged. "Sorry Barkley, but our walk to visit the general will have to wait until tomorrow. Let's go inside and find Nellie."

17

THE ADVANTAGE OF DOUBT

Mary's impatience for more information was growing to levels of desperation when through the drawing room window she saw Cook ambling up the driveway to the house.

"I must have a word with Cook before she disappears below-stairs with your servants," Mary said to Nellie, who was quietly reading, driving Mary to distraction, for she hadn't said a word since Mary joined her in the drawing room just a short while ago.

Nellie looked up, apparently surprised Mary was in the room. She made eye contact, nodded, and then returned to her book.

Outside the drawing room, in the entrance hall, Mary found Cook chatting amiably with the maid who'd opened the door for her.

"Oh, Cook," Mary said lightly. "Can we converse before you retire for the night?"

"Certainly, milady." Cook grinned.

The maid disappeared below-stairs, and Mary took Cook upstairs to her room.

"I don't want anyone to overhear." Mary closed the door

behind Cook. "Particularly not the girls, until I'm sure we have something to tell."

"There's not a lot to tell, milady," Cook replied. "All the gentlemen we're interested in like smoked bacon, and both Beacham and Illingsworth like oysters. None of the men care for olives or any of the suggested vegetables. They like meat and Gentleman's Relish, so far as I'm able to discover."

Mary laughed. "My late husband, may he rest in peace, was the same."

"That General Lowther does like kedgeree for breakfast and some other dishes I've never heard of," Cook said. "And Mr. Marmalade likes devils on horseback, but not often for breakfast, so the cook here says."

"Did Beacham's cook offer any ideas on why the police were looking for leftover wrappers?"

"She says they're crazy," Cook said. "Would a murderer poison someone with food and throw the wrapper or container in the bin?"

Mary nodded. "A question we've all asked ourselves, and yet we've no other way of finding out who poisoned Beacham when we now know it must have been in the food."

"She did say Mr. Beacham was a wicked man, sleeping around the way he did," Cook added.

"Sounds like she had a strong church background as a girl," Mary said.

"I got that impression, so I asked the others later, but they say if she had, it doesn't appear often in her life today."

Mary laughed. "So we can't see her as a wronged mistress wreaking vengeance on an unfaithful lover."

Cook smiled. "I think not, milady. She isn't the sort to catch the eye of someone like Beacham."

"No," Mary said. "As in art, I think Beacham saw himself as a connoisseur of female beauty, and his cook, Miss Harbottle, doesn't fit that picture."

"And besides," Cook said. "She is older than Beacham, and he appears to like younger women."

"Though his conquests we know of around here are his own age or thereabouts, not older."

"None of them are even a year older than him," Cook stated flatly, not caring to have her judgment dismissed. "He was very traditional that way."

"Did anything pop out that we haven't heard before? For instance," Mary continued, somewhat tentatively, "what exactly did the Marmalades' staff say when you asked where Mr. and Mrs. Marmalade were that morning?"

"Nothing new in that direction, milady. I asked them all what they did earlier that morning," Cook said. "They were all preparing breakfast, they say, except Beacham's cook. Both Beacham and Mrs. Beacham had already left the house, so Miss Harbottle had breakfast alone in her room, there being no other live-in staff to feed."

"She has no alibi, then, but also no motive," Mary said. "Or none we know of anyway. Thank you, Cook, that was excellent sleuthing on your part. Now I just need to hear from Ponsonby about developments in London."

And I need to investigate Nellie myself. My assistants won't bring the required rigor to the search. And there's Beacham's cook again, or to be exact, the confirmation of her location that morning.

LATE THAT EVENING, the phone rang in Mary's room. She snatched it up, almost sending it flying across the room. She'd been waiting all evening for Ponsonby's call.

"I have little to report," Ponsonby told her. "However, I've only just started. Tomorrow morning when everything is open around the gallery, I may have more success. I sought out the artist, but I'm afraid he's too far gone into drugs to be a credible witness."

"Keep me informed," Mary replied. "Whenever you have something new to share." She hung up the phone, not yet despondent but aware people didn't share incriminating evidence with strangers in a big city. Ponsonby would need his wits about him to make headway.

Sleep was a long time coming that night.

MORNING BROUGHT A SUNNY DAY, and Mary's spirits rose. On a morning like this, anything was possible. She would interview General Lowther, then phone Inspector Acton and try to extract information from him, particularly on the progress of his investigation. It puzzled her that, after the release of Gerry and the searching through local waste bins, they'd heard nothing more from him.

Mary laid out her schedule for the day, then went downstairs. *Nellie's cook had once again outdone herself.* Mary had just finished selecting her breakfast from the buffet when Dotty crept silently into the room.

"Lady Mary," Dotty murmured.

"Yes?" Mary sighed—her few minutes of quiet were gone.

"I have something to tell you that I don't want to tell you and wish I didn't have to tell you, but I must," Dotty said in one breathless string of words.

"This must be serious." Mary smiled.

Dotty inclined her head. "It is. Though, I'm sure it's entirely innocent, because if it isn't, then one of us may be implicated in the murder."

"Tell me."

"As you know, we, Winnie and I, have been here staying with Margie on and off all summer."

"Yes?"

"I've been thinking a lot about the whole series of odd events, and last night, I realized something I don't like, but I think you should know."

"Dotty," Mary said slowly, trying not to show her frustration. "Just tell me. Let me judge for myself if it's significant or not."

"Margie wasn't home when some of the odd incidents happened. Not the puncture, that seems to be solved, but the car damage and..." She hesitated. "The two animal poisonings."

Surprised, Mary asked, "Are you sure?"

Dotty nodded unhappily. "I thought and thought and tested my memory, and in the end, yes, I'm sure."

"But it was Margie who brought the odd incidents to my attention. She wouldn't do that if she was the one doing them, surely? It gives me a horrible feeling," Mary agreed. "I can't believe it, but we must find out where Margie went during those absences. Can you do it without involving Winnie?"

"It will be hard," Dotty said. "Because I don't know who I can ask."

"Has Margie gone 'absent without leave' since the murder?"

"Yesterday, when we were out interviewing the shopkeepers, Margie was last to return, and she wasn't where she should've been when we looked for her."

Dissension in the ranks? That is unexpected. "How long was she out of your sight?"

"Half an hour, at least," Dotty said. "I've been wondering if another odd occurrence will show up soon."

"Did she say where she'd been?"

Dotty shook her head. "Only that she'd been delayed with the witnesses."

"Sounds like you had a rotten night," Mary said sympathetically.

"I did," Dotty replied. "I'm sure none of this means anything bad, but I can't explain it."

I don't like it, but I fear we must investigate. "Today, I'll send you all out doing more interviews, on who likes smoky bacon or olives for breakfast, maybe. You suggest splitting up and then follow Margie and see where she goes and what she does," Mary said.

Mary sent the girls out with this new mission, then took it upon herself to look over the general's property and, if possible, talk to him.

General Lowther was easy to find. He was patrolling the perimeter of his property, a good-sized garden that included a small orchard.

"A beautiful morning," Mary called brightly.

"It is indeed, madam," the old man said with grave formality.

Mary deduced he wasn't used to strange women hailing him, nor at all pleased to find it happening.

"I'm admiring your garden," she said. "You have it laid out beautifully, and so well-tended. I can see you're a passionate gardener."

He smiled. "I'm afraid I can't take credit for this garden; I inherited it when I bought the property, but I do love it. You should've seen the garden I had in India. Planted it myself. It was a riot of color and scent all year round." He paused. "Well, not in the monsoon season, of course, but the way it flourished from the moment the deluge ended took my breath away."

"I'm surprised you could leave it," Mary said.

"Oh," the general said sadly. "I couldn't stay. Gandhi was

right; India was theirs to run, whatever the outcome. I felt it best to come back to my own land and make it a better place."

"Well, in your garden, you certainly have," Mary replied, pleased she'd broken through the stiff reserve of the initial few moments.

"I like to think I'm doing the original gardener proud."

"You are. I'm staying at the Marmalades'," Mary said. "We've just had a reminder that not everything is perfect in the garden, in a manner of speaking."

He nodded. "There are always pests, even in the best of gardens. And my allusion is very apt in this case."

"You didn't like Mr. Beacham?"

"Couldn't abide the fellow," Lowther said. "He was a crook of the worst kind. I've no doubt they'll find a disgruntled client who killed him. Could have done so myself at one time."

Mary laughed. "But not this time?"

He grinned sheepishly and shook his head. "I was a soldier for all my life, but in my personal life, I'm a peaceable man. He robbed me; I've no doubt, but that's what you get for trusting a neighbor instead of going to an independent expert."

"He sold something for you?"

"He did, and I got about a quarter of what I should've received," Lowther said, "according to an Indian artifacts expert I spoke to later."

"You didn't go to court?"

"Lawyers would have taken me for more than Beacham did," Lowther replied. "No, I chalked it up to experience and never went through him again."

"You're fortunate you have things to sell," Mary said. "So many people are struggling even this long after the war."

"I'd rather have kept them. They reminded me so much of a time and place I loved."

"You have no suspicions about Beacham's death?"

"None at all. He was an odious little tick, and the world is better off without him. If you want to know who did it, you should ask about his clients and his string of women friends. What do women see in such people . . . Oh, and consider their husbands. It's a wide field, and any one of them would have just cause."

"Heavens," Mary exclaimed. "I had no idea. Who were his female friends?"

Lowther guffawed. "You'd be better asking who weren't his paramours."

"Did you see him with any?"

"Not as such," Lowther admitted. "He was very discreet."

"Then you only know what you've been told?"

He shook his head. "Not exactly. I walk my dog along the track behind the new houses along the west road. I'd often see him along the path on my way out, and a different woman walking away on my way back. Like I said, discreet. Never together."

"Who were these women?"

"Wives and servants from the village," Lowther said.

"Such as?"

Lowther frowned. "I'm not giving you any names. For all I know, they were all out for a stroll along the path and nothing to do with him. It would be very wrong to cast aspersions on potentially innocent people."

He seems like an honest man. "But you don't believe they were innocent."

"Of course not. We're all adults here. There were too many to be coincidences."

"What about the morning he died?" Mary asked. "Were you walking your dog that morning?"

He raised his eyebrows and nodded.

"Did you see Beacham along that track?"

"I did but, before you ask, I didn't see any women that morning." His expression was honest.

"That's interesting," Mary said. *Is the fact he didn't see a woman that day significant?* "Tell me, did you always see a woman when you saw Beacham on that path?"

He shook his head. "Usually, but not always, no."

Mary thanked him, and they exchanged a few more pleasantries about gardening and the difficulty of getting good gardeners. She returned to the Marmalades' home, considering what she'd learned.

Beacham often made the trip to that shed, and women were often seen on the path coming away from that direction. It's suggestive but hardly damning evidence.

I hope Dotty finds a reason for Margie's absence that isn't criminal. Rose thought Nellie was Beacham's other woman, and Nellie and Margie both blush when we talk of Beacham's secret assignations. Oh, pother! I don't like where this is going at all.

18

THE NET TIGHTENS

Mary told Ponsonby of Dotty's forebodings when he phoned to report on his morning's results.

"There's likely a simple explanation," Ponsonby replied. "Miss Marjorie is as honest as the day is long."

"I agree." *I certainly hope she has her wits about her.* She sighed. "But we must take it seriously in any case."

"I suggest those young men she didn't want to interview will be at the root of it, or at least one of them will be."

Mary laughed. "I fear you may be right. Nellie would be horrified if she found out. Still, I hope when the girls return, Dotty will have an answer." She explained how she'd set Dotty the task of watching Margie this morning.

"I have every confidence Margie will be exonerated," Ponsonby said. "If not today, then subsequently."

"Even if the explanation is as simple as we think, can we trust a young woman who isn't honest about her affections for a young man?"

Though, I find this very hard to believe. I will be sad to learn I can't trust the dear girl.

"My lady, with first loves, there's always a fear of others

knowing. Parental objection, friends' dislike of our choice, and just a wish to be secret until we understand it ourselves, is enough to promote secrecy," Ponsonby replied in his best butler voice. "My faith in Miss Margie will be undiminished, even if I disapprove of her choice."

Mine also, I admit, though I fear for her reputation.

"But can we also dismiss the coincidence of their trysts aligning with certain odd events?"

"That is harder to ignore," Ponsonby agreed. "Though I think we should group the incidents into three categories. First, and least significant, are the punctures. Second are the burglary and car issues, and whether cars could have been tampered with, and third is the killing of the two animals.

"Now," Mary asked, "what did you learn this morning?"

"I learned Winkler's neighbors don't like him very much," Ponsonby said. "Sadly, none of them can say he was out on his motorcycle on the day of the murder, though I think they would like to."

Mary laughed. "Good, anything more about that artist?"

"Just that he doesn't know anything about Winkler's movements."

"So nothing to say he was, or wasn't, in Upper Wainbury that morning," Mary said thoughtfully. "He's still on my list of suspects."

"I'll keep interviewing people here, but I'm not sure we're going to learn anything here in London," Ponsonby said. "Most people only knew Beacham as a man who came to the shop and gallery once in a while. There are no friends I can discover or even recent business acquaintances."

"He might have girlfriends," Mary said. "He had enough down here."

"I'll ask. Now here's what I'm doing this afternoon."

After Ponsonby outlined his plans, Mary ended the call.

Smiling, she prepared to descend the stairs for lunch. Ponsonby's avuncular affection for her three assistants was a constant source of delight. However, his certainty of Margie's innocence made her uncomfortable that she was wavering on it. *Please let Dotty have good news.*

The three young sleuths were already home and wolfing down plates of food from the lunch buffet when Mary entered the room. She greeted them and suggested they don't report on their findings until they could be alone after lunch. Nellie or Gerry may enter the room at any moment, and she knew the working of fate—someone would be in the middle of a sentence the parents would want explained.

With lunch over, they retired to deck chairs on the lawn, where they could talk freely and stop if anyone approached. The reports were all negative. Nothing new had been learned.

"Then, ladies, I suggest you dress for tennis or some other summer activity while this beautiful weather continues," Mary said.

Margie and Winnie agreed. Dotty said she was too full and would join them later.

"You shouldn't be so greedy." Winnie laughed.

"I have a healthy appetite, and, anyway, the doctor says I need to maintain my strength. Apparently, I'm frail."

"In what way?" Margie mocked. "You look pretty plump to us."

"I don't know," Dotty replied crossly. "It's what our doctor says."

Margie and Winnie skipped off to the house, leaving Dotty and Mary alone.

"Well?" Mary asked. "Did you follow her?"

Dotty leaned in, her voice low. "She met one of the young men. The most loutish of the lot, I'd say. It was shocking."

Mary laughed with relief. "We all have infatuations that aren't quite what our friends would wish."

"Her parents would have a fit."

Mary nodded, still smiling. "Which explains her secrecy." Soaring with happiness.

"And that she's making a complete fool of herself," Dotty added.

"Perhaps, but now we need to know why her trysts with that boy coincide with those odd events. We also need to know if this boy has enemies. Is there someone who wanted the incidents linked to him to remove him from the village, or just from Margie, maybe?" Mary mused.

"I've only just found him," Dotty said hotly. "I couldn't discover all that this morning."

"You misunderstand me, my dear," Mary said. "I was wondering aloud, not casting aspersions on your detective work, which is exemplary."

"Oh. Sorry. Should I look into those things? Margie might see me and know she was being watched today."

"You're right," Mary said. "Leave it to me. I'm sure the adults will know, just as soon as we know his name."

"His first name is Enoch," Dotty said. "Really, she couldn't get more *Cold Comfort Farm* if she'd tried."

Mary laughed. "But it's a name the parents will know. If it had been Tom, Dick, or Harry, there could be a dozen of them in the neighborhood."

"In this neighborhood, there could be a dozen Enochs," Dotty said gloomily. "Really, it's beyond the back of beyond."

Once Dotty returned to the others, and they'd made their way to the tennis court, Mary found Nellie having coffee and Gerry smoking his pipe in the drawing room and broached the subject of Enoch.

"He's Ted Cutler's son," Gerry replied at once. "Farms over

on the valley side, down Bottomley way." Bottomley was the village immediately west of Upper Wainbury. "He's a nice lad, always willing to lend a hand when one is needed."

Nellie's expression suggested she didn't entirely agree with her husband.

"Nellie?" Mary asked.

Nellie acted flustered. "Oh, Enoch's all right in his way. He'll do well when he takes over the farm from his father, I've no doubt. But he isn't the sort of boy I'd want Margie to spend time with. They're a rough lot, those Cutlers."

Gerry laughed. "Just horseplay, my dear. Young lads letting off steam. There's no harm in it."

"Is there something specific you're referring to?" Mary asked.

Nellie answered. "There's often trouble after closing at the local pub, and Enoch's name invariably comes up."

"Has he been arrested?"

Gerry laughed again. "Constable Watkins knows there's no harm in it. He settles them down and sends them home. Like I said, young men having fun on a Saturday night. A story as old as there's been men and pubs, and before, too, I've no doubt."

"There's no suggestion this fun included sabotaging cars?" Mary asked.

"None at all," Gerry replied.

"Has Constable Watkins investigated any of the incidents?"

Nellie shook her head. "They all looked like normal events. Tires do get punctures, particularly if nails are dropped on the road by careless construction workers. One of the car issues seemed like a nut on the brake lines had worked loose, but there's no evidence someone loosened it. And so on."

"Except the cat and dog," Mary said.

"But the dog was a favorite of all the village children when they were growing up. None of them would've poisoned it. The cat, now . . ." Gerry broke off.

"Does Enoch have any enemies?"

"Look here," Gerry cried, suddenly frowning. "What are you insinuating about Enoch? Why all this interest?"

Mary was ready with her reply. "The girls saw him striding around in the village, and one of them said he was the 'loutiest lout of the lot.' It started me thinking, but I admit it may have colored my thinking as well."

"He's a big half-grown boy," Nellie said. "He'll be right enough when he's finished growing. He may look like a lout to our city slickers, but he'll look very well soon enough. Don't hold his present unruly appearance against him."

Mary laughed. "Well, if he's caught your eye, Nellie, I'll certainly be sure to look for him when I'm next in the village."

Nellie shook her head but was red in the face.

Mary moved the subject on to tomorrow and her plans.

"What I want to hear is the police have arrested the killer," Gerry said. "It's annoying we hear nothing from them but see them around the village every day. They can't still be looking for the packaging they talked about yesterday."

"You're a justice of the peace, Gerry," Mary said. "Why not ask them?"

Gerry's expression darkened. "I have, but they say I'm not yet off their suspect list, so they're not sharing anything with me. I'm not sure I will be able to treat Inspector Acton's cases honestly in the future."

"It can't be that bad, Gerry," Mary said.

"Oh, isn't it, though?" Gerry snapped. "It's back to 1945 again. I'm the one pushing for justice, and I'm the one everyone suspects."

Mary saw at once this case had genuinely reawakened Gerry's horror at the way he'd been treated all those years ago, and it added a new insult to the old injury. He couldn't help her.

"I'll phone Acton right now," Mary said. "On the phone in

the hall." Gerry's expression, which had relaxed a little, settled back into despair she'd never seen in him before. "It's best Acton thinks I'm alone."

The inspector answered the phone at once, which took Mary by surprise. She explained her call, and he listened in silence.

"Lady Mary," Acton said when she'd finished speaking. "I've heard from people in Scotland Yard you have had some success in solving mysteries."

"I have, and I'm anxious to help here."

"I'd normally never allow a member of the public to be involved," Acton began, "but I'd welcome a different pair of eyes on this evidence."

"I could be at the station in minutes," Mary said, her spirits lifting.

"There's a condition," Acton said. "And it may cause you some difficulty. I must ask you not to share anything with Mr. Marmalade."

"I understand, Inspector. It's not doing your relationship with the Marmalades any good either, though."

Acton laughed. "My relationship with Mr. Marmalade is professional. He's a JP, and I'm a police detective. We're often at odds. It's the nature of things. Yours is one of friendship and not so easy to smooth over."

"From what I was told, I'm confident I can trust you. Now, if you wish to give us the results of your investigations, we'll show you ours."

"I'll do that when I get there," Mary said, "which will be about fifteen minutes. I hope, when we share what we've learned, between us we may see the truth, or at least a light at the end of the tunnel."

"I hope so too," Acton replied. "But I fear it may not bode well for your friends."

19

RALLY FOR TRUTH

Mary pulled the Rolls into a parking spot designated for Inspector Acton. Striding purposefully into the station, she was promptly ushered into Acton's office, where she began by explaining her choice of parking, her tone a mix of apology and jest. Acton's laughter, unexpected but genuine, echoed in the room.

"Deliberately provocative or just laziness?" He smiled.

"Neither. It just made sense. Now, can we begin?" When he nodded his agreement, Mary said, "I'll start."

She quickly outlined the discoveries she and her companions had made. She held certain points back, reserved for future trading.

"Thank you." He gestured for her to follow. "Come with me."

Mary fell into step behind him, and they entered a room brimming with activity, tables strewn with potential evidence and blackboards with chalk diagrams and notes—painting a vivid picture of the investigation's intensity.

Amid this organized chaos, Mary moved with purpose through the array of items found by the police in their searches, her keen eye honing in on certain items.

She pointed decisively at the card-shaped tin that lay before them. Her voice held a hint of intrigue as she questioned, "This fish can. What was in it, and where did you find it?"

"Oysters in linseed oil and at the Beacham house."

Mary's lips curved into a knowing smile. "They do say oysters are an aphrodisiac. Maybe he believed it, and maybe it's accurate."

Acton's grin mirrored her sentiment, his amusement evident. "He certainly put himself about a lot," he concurred. "For such an ordinary-looking man, he was a true Casanova."

"So I've been hearing. There's no accounting for lust, is there?"

"It seems not."

Mary met his gaze. "None, but I've only just started."

"What do you make of this?" Acton picked up a gold chain necklace with green stones—dangling the pendant between his fingers.

Mary scrutinized it with a sharp analytical gaze. She leaned in. "A rich woman's necklace." Her fingers twitched with the urge to touch, but she resisted. "If that's real gold, and emeralds."

"Both of those are true," Acton said. "Now why do you think a woman who lost this didn't ask for police help to find it? It's worth a lot of money, our experts say. My annual salary, to be precise."

Her brows pinched, her mind deep in concentration. "She doesn't know she's lost it, or she wouldn't dare admit it because it could have been lost somewhere incriminating."

Acton's expression remained pensive. "Do you know whose it is?"

"I've never seen it, so no, I don't know," Mary admitted, frustrated. "Do you have any leads?"

"Sadly, I don't yet. Today, I plan to interview all the wealthier women in the village and ask if it's theirs. When they say 'no,' which they will, I'll tell them I'm asking the same question of their husbands tomorrow."

Mary's eyes widened in amusement. "Well, that certainly should stir things up."

His eyes twinkled. "A little disruption can often lead to revealing truths, I find."

"May I ask where it was found?"

"I think you can guess," Acton replied. "You said that you and your butler searched the place before us. By the way, did you find anything? This would be a good time to mention it, if you did."

"We didn't find anything, but we didn't have the time," Mary said. "Where did you find this?"

Acton uncrossed his arms. "It had fallen into the crack between two floor planks and was almost invisible from above or below."

"I wish we had found it," Mary said. "We could have found the owner easier than you."

"I think not. The woman who lost this knows where she likely lost it and probably knows when. The morning of the murder, most likely. We find the owner of this, and we have our murderer, or should I say, murderess."

Mary continued examining the finds from the police search. They'd been most diligent, and it had taken some time. Almost at the end lay a small plastic sword of the sort used to skewer hors d'oeuvres.

"Is this from the shed too?" she asked.

"No, but on the path nearby. Why?"

"I've been considering the hiding of a sedative in strong-tasting foods, and something like *angels on horseback* was one of them. This little skewer would fit that possibility."

"Your guess is correct," Acton said. "Bacon and oysters, it was."

"Did you find any home where that was prepared that morning?" Mary asked eagerly.

"None of the cooks admit to making bacon and oysters that morning, and none of the people in those houses say they had such a dish that morning, which leaves us with a real clue we can't yet capitalize on."

"We must find the owner of that necklace," Mary said. "It's very distinctive, and someone will remember it. Can I show it to my three assistants?"

Acton considered for a moment. "Very well, bring them to my office, and they can view it there. I'm not sharing all our finds with your assistants."

ON HER WAY HOME, Mary saw Mrs. Jenkins, the Marmalades' cook, entering the butcher's shop. She quickly parked the car and strolled nonchalantly, she hoped, back toward the shop. Slowing her pace, looking in windows, she timed her arrival at the butcher's shop doorway to when the cook came out.

"Hello," Mary said as Mrs. Jenkins stepped out of the door. "What are we having tonight for dinner?" She gestured to the basket Jenkins carried.

"This isn't for us, Your Grace. These are bones for Barkley. He has a healthy appetite."

Mary laughed. "I'm trying to slim him down."

"There's no fat on bones," Jenkins replied. "In fact, these will help your attempts to lower his weight."

"I'm sure they will." Mary smiled. "By the way, I've been meaning to ask something about the morning of Mr. Beacham's death." She invited Jenkins to walk with her with a flourish of her hand.

"What about that morning?"

"I'm sure you've answered this question a number of times these past days," Mary said. "But I want to be sure. I hear everything secondhand, you see."

"It must be difficult, just talking to people when you're a duchess."

"It can be. I know there was quite a gathering that morning, getting ready for the tennis tournament, so it's probably hard for you to remember where everyone was."

"Not hard at all," Mrs. Jenkins replied. "Mrs. Yelland was there, and Alice—Mrs. Marmalade's maid...and I was there in the kitchen, oh, and Miss Harbottle joined us later."

"You were all in the kitchen all the time?"

"Most of the time. Alice was in and out, setting the table and so on, of course."

"Of course, and Mr. and Mrs. Marmalade, did they look in?" Mary hoped she wasn't making it all too obvious.

"No. Mr. Marmalade was out after breakfast, and Mrs. Marmalade would be upstairs, probably in her room getting ready, though she didn't call for Alice to help her dress." Mrs. Jenkins's expression was suddenly puzzled.

"If Nellie's anything like me," Mary said quickly, "she'll have been pulling every dress she had out of the closet and trying and discarding them until she found one she was happy with. Only then do I call my maid."

Mrs. Jenkins brightened. "I expect you're right. She was quite nervous about the tournament. Probably because of the high-jinks last year." She paused, then smiled. "Or maybe because she was having a duchess to stay."

Mary chortled. "Nellie and I were at school together. She knows enough about me not to be nervous."

Mrs. Jenkins stopped. "I need to finish my shopping. Was there anything else I can help you with?"

"Nothing, thank you, Mrs. Jenkins," Mary replied. "You've set my mind at rest, and that's all I needed."

When Jenkins was safely inside the greengrocer's, Mary walked back to the car, her mind troubled. *So neither Gerry nor Nellie can be accounted for that morning. I have to ask them directly; there's no other way of confirming their whereabouts.*

WHEN MARY BROUGHT the girls to view the necklace in Acton's office, she was pleased to see Margie's shock.

"Well, Margie?" Mary asked.

"I think it's Rose Illingsworth's necklace. I'm sure I've seen it before."

"Can you swear to that?" Acton asked.

"No," Margie said seriously. "But I think I'm right."

"Ladies," Acton said. "Say nothing about this to anyone. We will reinterview Mrs. Illingsworth today and ask her if she recognizes this necklace. I want this to be a surprise."

"Thank you for allowing us to identify this necklace, Inspector," Mary said as he accompanied them to the door.

He laughed. "I realized it would be the quickest way to get the owner identified, so I was happy to have the help. We'd have struggled to get it identified in a close-knit society like Upper Wainbury. No one would want to snitch on their friends or their employer."

Mary and her assistants left the police station in silence—broken only when they felt safe to talk.

"Are you really sure, Margie?" Winnie asked. "You've put Mrs. Illingsworth in a lot of trouble if you aren't."

"I considered that," Margie said. "In the end, I felt sure

enough to say what I said. It's quite a distinctive piece of jewelry, but I don't think it can be very valuable."

"Why?" Mary asked.

"Because she wore it a lot. Mama keeps her real valuables only for special occasions."

Mary raised her eyebrows. "We all do. But I examined the necklace quite closely this morning, and I consider it extremely valuable."

Dotty frowned. "The fact she didn't alert anyone about its disappearance means she knew she lost it somewhere incriminating."

"I fear so," Mary said. "I think she lost it that morning, or at the very least the day before, because the murder is the most frightening event to prevent her telling anyone. If it had been weeks before, she'd have gone back to find it or made it known she'd lost it, and may even have offered a reward for its return."

"Oh dear," Winnie said. "I rather like Mrs. Illingsworth."

"It may turn out to be entirely innocent," Mary reminded her. "It's too early to begin worrying. Say nothing to anyone." *If it is Rose, it will be a great relief to me. Nellie is looming larger and larger in my mind.*

Back at the house, Mary found Nellie in the garden and took the opportunity to ask the question she wanted a reassuring answer on. "Nellie, I'm sure the police asked you this, but I'd like to know too. Were you here at the house all morning on the day of Beacham's murder?"

Nellie went pale. "You think I met and poisoned him?"

"Of course not," Mary replied. "I just want to be sure I have everyone's whereabouts that morning clear in my mind."

"I was here all morning," Nellie responded crossly. "Gerry, of course, had disappeared—just like a man to vanish when you need him—so I was here organizing everything."

Mary put on a positive expression. "I can imagine. Making sure the food preparation was on track and the tables set, seeing to the flowers and the drinks and glasses. A hostess's work is never done."

Nellie looked mollified. "My staff are excellent, but you have to keep on top of things, or mistakes happen."

"There were none that morning—everything went like clockwork," Mary said. "So you can vouch for the whereabouts of your staff too?"

"As I told the police."

Mary changed the topic. Any more questions about that morning would make Nellie suspicious. As they talked of old times, Mary's mind ran riot.

Nellie says she was checking her staff. Mrs. Jenkins says she didn't see her. Whom do I believe? Did the police pick up on this discrepancy, and if so, why haven't they questioned Nellie again?

As promised, Ponsonby phoned in his report later that evening, when he was confident no one else would pick up the call. Lady Mary picked it up in her bedroom.

"I have good news, my lady," Ponsonby said.

"From Beacham's business associates?" Mary asked.

"I'm afraid not. Either he's been out of their circle so long they have no idea of his business dealings or they're in on it. Either way, they claim to know nothing. No, my good news comes from Winkler's nearest neighbor, who does remember him leaving the house early on the morning of the murder."

"How can they be sure?"

"They'd arrived back from a trip that night very late. There were delays with trains and ferries, apparently, and they'd only just fallen asleep when Winkler's motorbike started, and it drove off down the street. They were very angry, as I'm sure we can all imagine."

"How early?" Mary asked. "Don't forget, Beacham was poisoned about seven thirty in the morning."

"They say it was four o'clock in the morning when he left," Ponsonby replied. "He would have to ride fast to be there, but it could be done. There's little traffic on the roads anywhere at that time of the morning."

"That is wonderful news," Mary said. "Perhaps ask him about it tomorrow morning and then return here?"

"That was my intention, my lady," Ponsonby said. "I'll be at his house when he leaves and then go straight to the rail station."

"Phone here when you know what time you're arriving, and someone will pick you up at the station."

"If I can, I will, but I'd be equally happy to walk from the station," Ponsonby said. "Anything to shake the smells of the city from my person. Soot and the smell of the river aren't the best colognes for anyone to wear."

Mary laughed. "Tomorrow, then, and here's hoping our art dealer just confesses, for I find we have more suspects now than when we started." She hung up and sat on her bed, smiling broadly.

Another happy finding to add to a glorious day. Margie was simply inappropriately seeing a young man, and now Beacham's business partner could well be the killer. All my fears about Nellie, Gerry and Margie are melting away like mist in the summer sun. It looks bad for Rose Illingsworth, whether she is the murderer or not, because her husband will soon learn where her necklace was found.

20

A STRONG FOREHAND, MAYBE

The following morning, Mary brought the team together in the library to discuss their most recent findings, at least the ones that could be shared—keeping Dotty's suspicions about Margie, and her suspicions about Nellie, to herself until she'd discovered which events tied into Margie's meetings with Enoch and whether Nellie had been where she said she was.

"First," Mary said when they'd all settled down, "Ponsonby has discovered Beacham's business partner could have been here in Upper Wainbury around seven thirty that morning, which means we need to find someone who heard the bike or saw the man that morning."

The girls groaned. "We've already asked everyone this," Margie said dejectedly. "Nobody heard the motorbike that morning."

"Then we must ask about the man," Mary said. "Someone might have seen a stranger, or a man they knew to be Beacham's partner, in the village that morning."

"They would have mentioned it," Winnie said. "Beacham wasn't very popular, so anything that reflected badly on him, like entertaining strangers at seven o' clock in the morning, would be commented on."

"Maybe the person who saw it didn't think it was strange," Mary said. "We must ask."

Mary switched tracks. "Cook, I have a job for you. Find out where in the village plastic skewers for food items can be bought and who bought them recently."

"What sort of skewers?" Cook asked.

"Here." Mary handed over a sheet of paper with a sword-shaped skewer drawn on it. "I drew this at the police station because I think it holds the key to this whole affair."

Cook took it. "Skewers of that sort are right here in this house. Every cocktail that's served has a cherry or an olive on one of those skewers. They're likely in every other house too."

"Perhaps," Mary said. "And maybe not. If we knew houses they weren't in, that might narrow the place where Beacham had his last meal down to a smaller number than the whole village."

"What will you be doing, Lady Mary?" Dotty asked.

"I have some avenues I want to explore this morning that may not lead anywhere but must be followed." Mary hoped Dotty wouldn't press any further because it was Dotty's revelation about Margie that Mary planned to confirm.

* * * * * * * * * * *

Taking the Rolls, Mary drove down to the Cutler farm, where she hoped to find Enoch alone. She was deep in thought as she drove round a short wall separating the narrow country road from a farmyard, and she found him—driving his tractor straight at the Rolls.

"Stop!" Mary yelled, as much to herself as to Enoch.

She slammed on the brakes. The tractor rolled to a stop. *Thank heavens he saw me and stopped as well.*

Leaving the car blocking the farm entranceway, Mary stepped out and approached the tractor. Peering up at Enoch, she shielded her eyes from the sun.

"What are you doing?" he yelled down, the churning of the tractor's engine nearly drowning him out. "I have work to do. Move your car." He waved his hand dramatically, as if he could move the car himself with the gesture.

"I will if you answer my questions," Mary shouted.

"What?" he yelled, and then cut the engine of the tractor.

Thank you. Perhaps we'll be able to hear each other now. "I said, I need you to answer some questions."

He clambered out of the tractor, his back bowed, and wiped his brow on a dirty rag.

"When you see Margie," Mary began, and had to wave her hand to stop his denial, "odd incidents have occurred in the village. Are you behind them?"

"Don't be stupid," Enoch said scornfully. "If I was with Margie, we were busy, and, anyway, she would have to be in on them too."

"Then do you have someone who dislikes you so much, they'd watch your movements and carry out these pranks when you couldn't account for your own movements?"

"But all it would take is Margie saying she was with me, if she was," Enoch replied.

"You know she'd struggle with that, and the prankster might know that too, maybe relied on it to get you into trouble."

Enoch considered this carefully. "Look, you're completely wrong about this. These pranks, as you call them—though they weren't really jokes, were they? Loosened brake lines, poisoned animals, burglaries aren't activities to be ignored, and they may have been discovered when I hadn't an alibi, but they were set in motion long before that. Even if the timing does appear when I'm not about—and I noticed that too—the setting of them wouldn't have been."

"You and Margie didn't see anything odd going on when you were together?"

"Margie will put you straight. She and I are never together. We were friendly at junior school, but she's gone to finishing school now and couldn't possibly be seen with me."

"Well, let me ask the question this way," Mary said, her tone gentle yet probing. "During the moments when you were out of sight of everyone else, did you notice anything you now find suspicious?"

Enoch shook his head, his uncertainty evident.

"Please," Mary implored. "If there's even the slightest inkling of something amiss, please, share it with me."

"It's not suspicious, but that morning, the one of the murder, when I was out in the pasture, rounding up some cows that weren't coming in for milking as quickly as I wanted, I heard a cry, just one. It was a woman's voice, but I couldn't see anyone."

"Where was this?"

"In the upper field near our sheds. I walked up the footpath" —he pointed to the line of the path climbing the valley side, from what Mary now knew to be the Cutler farm, marked out by hedgerows—"and entered the field by the gate at the sheds."

"Did you recognize the voice?"

He shook his head.

"A young woman?" Mary asked.

Enoch shook his head. "Not young but not old."

"And you saw no one," Mary said.

"Close when I entered through the gate but not near as I walked down the field back to our farm," Enoch said. "Look, it's likely just someone out for a walk and having a fright. Saw a snake or something like that."

"When was this?"

"I said, the morning of the murder. It wasn't a cry of distress, you understand, or I'd have tried to help."

"A cry but not of distress," Mary mused. "Anything else?"

"No," Enoch said.

"Do you know why Mr. Beacham rented space from your father in that new shed?"

"To keep his stock in," Enoch replied. "He said he bought items at auction that needed storing until his gallery could take them. But there wasn't any art stuff there whenever I looked in."

"What was there?"

"Not a lot. Some old furniture is all," Enoch replied.

"He sold collectible furniture as well as art," Mary said.

"Then maybe that's what I saw. An old bed frame, a chest of drawers, a rocking chair that looked Oriental, a mirror with a gilded frame, an old straight-backed chair, the sort we had in our schoolroom. None of it looked valuable to me. Just old junk."

As this described what she'd seen, Mary was sure he was truthful about this part of his evidence, at least.

"Thank you, Enoch. You've been most helpful. I see a whole new possibility opening up in my investigation."

"Investigation is the police's job," Enoch stated flatly, and started the tractor again to drown out any reply.

Well, that was rude!

Mary jumped in and backed the Rolls out of the gateway. Enoch roared by without a backward glance. Mary sighed. She had wanted to say she could talk to Margie's parents on his behalf but realized it would only raise false hopes. It may be 1958, but "finished" young ladies still didn't marry farmers, however prosperous they may one day become.

Mary arrived at the Marmalade house to be greeted by Nellie in an excited state, and Barkley, who'd caught Nellie's excitement.

"Have you heard?" Nellie demanded before Mary had a chance to greet her.

"What would I have heard?" Mary asked, petting Barkley's head as he tried to jump up and lick her face.

"The police have arrested Rose Illingsworth!"

"Oh dear," Mary said. "I do hope Inspector Acton has good evidence for that." *At least it wasn't Nellie.*

"Do you have a more likely murderer in mind?"

"No, not *more* likely," Mary replied. "But I could be wrong."

"Who is it?"

Mary shook her head. "I can't cast aspersions on people without proof, Nellie. That would be very wrong."

"I won't tell anyone," Nellie protested.

"Nellie, my dear, you would hint and suggest until everyone pressured you to say who, and you would." *And I can't tell you anything because I feel like you're involved.*

"I would not," Nellie cried, affronted.

"It doesn't matter what you would or would not do," Mary said. "I'm not saying anything until I'm sure, and that needs evidence and proof."

"I hope the police are right," Nellie said, aggrieved. "Then you'll look silly with all your talk about other people." She flounced off into the drawing room, leaving Mary wondering if she should follow or give Nellie time to cool off. Hearing her assistants in the billiard room was all she needed to hear, and her mind was made up.

"Have you heard the news?" Winnie shouted as Mary entered.

"Nellie just told me," Mary said. "What do you three think?"

"I think Margie got it right about that necklace," Dotty said. "And we solved the whole thing because of it."

The others laughed, telling Dotty she was exaggerating.

"Margie identified a necklace, but they must have more than that to arrest her," Mary said. "She could have lost it anytime."

"She practically admitted killing him," Margie said. "Their maid told our maid that Mrs. Illingsworth told Acton she'd wanted to kill Beacham for weeks."

"Still, wanting to kill someone isn't a crime," Mary replied. "Or many of us would be in jail."

"That's true," Winnie said. "The times I've wished cosmic death on my mother would have me jailed for life."

"Never mind that for now," Mary said. "What did you learn this morning?"

"Nothing," Margie cried. "As I told you before you sent us on the wild goose chase."

"It's true," Dotty said. "No one we talked to heard a motorbike in the early hours of that morning."

Mary frowned. "That only says he didn't bring the bike into the village. He may have parked it somewhere near the main road and walked. Did anyone see a stranger that morning?"

"No," Winnie said. "And we pushed them to remember."

"Were any of the people you spoke to out and about that morning?"

"Not really," Margie said. "They were preparing breakfast and things but not wandering the streets."

"The general might have seen him?" Mary mused.

"You said he hadn't seen anyone," Winnie reminded her.

Mary shook her head. "He said he hadn't seen a woman that morning. I should've asked about a man."

"Wouldn't he have said, if he'd seen a man?" Winnie asked.

"I asked directly about a woman," Mary replied. "His revelation was about the women he'd seen at that early hour, so I think he would assume it was a woman I was interested in."

"Phone him," Margie suggested. "His number will be in the phone book. I'll get it for you." Margie ran out of the room.

21

TOP SPIN OF TRUTH

Mary quickly followed her with the others close on her heels. By the time she was in her room, Margie was there with a phone book opened at the *B*s, pointing at Lowther's number. Mary dialed and waited. A gruff male voice answered. *The general.*

"Hmm," Lowther said thoughtfully when the question was put to him. "Not on the path, but I did see a man at the door of Beacham's house. I didn't recognize him. A small man, rather scrawny, but that could've just been his clothes. They were very heavy for a summer morning."

That must have been Winkler.

"You're sure you didn't recognize him?" Mary asked.

"I'm sure, but then I wasn't interested in who would call on Beacham," Lowther replied. "He'd be another crook, you can be sure, but the police wouldn't do anything if I told them someone had called on Beacham. It's not an offense to call on someone, even for crooks."

"Could you say what time?"

"When I was heading out," Lowther said. "So seven thirty-ish or thereabouts."

"You didn't see what came of his call? Was he shown into the house? Was the house empty and he left?" Mary asked, growing excited. *Why didn't Beacham's cook mention this? She was in the house, even if Fran and Cyril were off on a tryst.*

"I think the house must have been unoccupied," Lowther said slowly. "He was peering in the window when he passed out of my view."

"Did you see anyone in the fields that morning?" Mary asked.

"Enoch Cutler was herding cows down toward the farm but too far off to speak to."

"Thank you, General," Mary said. "That's most helpful."

"If it puts any of those rogues behind bars, I'm happy to help."

Mary hung up the phone. "Did you hear that?"

Her three sleuths clapped, their eyes sparkling with excitement.

"Beacham's partner could have been here when it happened," Mary said. "I'll phone Inspector Acton and have him follow up."

Acton, however, wasn't as enthusiastic about Mary's new information as he had been about Margie's identifying the necklace.

"I realize you're sure it's Mrs. Illingsworth, Inspector, but it's vitally important that this be followed up. I can give you all the background. You only need to confirm with our sources and press Beacham's partner harder."

Acton placated her and muttered, "Sure, sure. Good day, Lady Mary."

Mary replaced the phone. "Inspector Acton finds us a bit of a nuisance, I fear," Mary said to the others, who looked downcast.

"He should be pleased to have such help," Dotty said.

Mary smiled. "Professionals of all kinds find it hard to be

glad of help, even good help, from persons outside their area of expertise."

"He'll hate it even more if this information turns out to have unmasked the murderer," Winnie said.

"I fear you're right," Mary replied. "Now, I'm taking poor Barkley for a walk. He's anxious to go. I'm not sure how long he can hold it."

"We'll come too." Dotty jumped from her chair.

"Speak for yourself." Winnie slouched deeper into hers.

"Margie?" Mary inquired, amused at the indecision on Margie's face.

"I'll stay with Winnie," Margie said at last. "We can play snooker."

Barkley, Mary and Dotty left the house and proceeded to the footpath that led past the shed where they believed Beacham had been injected.

"It can't have been his business partner who murdered him," Dotty began, "unless he's"—she hesitated—"you know, that way."

"We're speculating on everything," Mary said. "Nothing has yet revealed the breakthrough we need."

"The police think they've solved it," Dotty said. "Did you get anything from your meeting with Enoch?"

"I did," Mary said. "You were right there—Margie and Enoch are seeing each other, though Enoch says they're not."

"Very childish," Dotty said loftily.

"We all are when we're in love," Mary replied. "What was even more interesting is Enoch said he heard a cry as he entered the gate near the shed. Only once, and a woman's voice. I wanted to retrace his steps from his farm to where he might have heard that cry."

"Why only one?" Dotty asked.

"Exactly," Mary said. "Enoch said he imagined a woman

startled by a snake or something, and that's possible, of course. But he also said it wasn't a cry that suggested she was in danger, and he continued with his job of herding the cows to the milking barn."

As they approached the shed, Barkley ran into the hedgerow and wriggled through a gap.

"Barkley," Mary commanded. "Come back at once."

Barkley wriggled back through the hedge and, trotting to her side, dropped a miniature plastic sword with shreds of white flesh, perhaps oyster, still attached. He eyed her as if to say "Now will you listen to me?"

Mary crouched and studied the remnants nature had left of what had undoubtedly been a bacon-wrapped oyster. "I'll take this to Inspector Acton. Maybe the police laboratory can get something from these remains."

"I can't think what." Dotty wrinkled her nose as Mary picked up the sword with her handkerchief and wrapped it before placing it in her jacket pocket.

"The police found something like this on the side of the path," she replied. "This may help tie the two together or identify what kind of oysters and bacon, and they can narrow down the houses from that. Who bought from the village shop and who from the butcher, for instance."

"Our murderer threw away the unfinished breakfast items as they left," Dotty said, still puzzled over this new evidence. "Do you think the police lab might find the sedative in the pieces on this skewer?"

"The murderer couldn't eat them. Even Barkley sensed something wrong with it, or he'd have gobbled the evidence, sword and all. They couldn't take the remnants of that last meal back to the house is my guess. As to the police lab identifying the sedative, I don't know."

"But who is the murderer?"

"Someone who knew Beacham's fondness of these items and who could make them and bring them to him here," Mary mused.

"They couldn't make them that morning, though." Dotty shook her head. "It would take too long, and the smell would arouse curiosity when they didn't appear on the breakfast table."

"Most homes have bacon for breakfast," Mary added. "Except General Lowther. He has kedgeree."

"Kedgeree has fish, so that too would've explained the smell if anyone asked," Dotty said.

"There's no one at the general's house to ask, and he wouldn't serve Beacham anything other than poison."

"But someone did serve Beacham poison," Dotty retorted.

"I think they must have been cooked earlier, perhaps the previous day, and some held back for this purpose," Mary said. "Then fifteen minutes reheating in the oven and, voilà, an aphrodisiac before the fun began."

"Except he would fall asleep," Dotty reminded Mary. "No fun that morning."

"I think there may have been some," Mary said. "It would take time for the sedative to work."

"Then the real point of the event followed?" Dotty asked.

"Yes, she injected him with enough nicotine for him to die slowly and away from this shed"—Mary pointed at the building they now stood before—"and away from her. It was clever and cruel."

"I don't like to speak ill of the dead," Dotty muttered. "But that's how many people have described Beacham."

"Quite," Mary said, and left, circumnavigating the shed. At the side facing the Cutler farm, she stopped and studied the siding. There was no window, but there were gaps in the planking. Had someone seen the approaching Enoch through one and stopped the game when they saw he'd heard a cry?

"Does Enoch whistle when he walks?" Mary asked. "Many men do."

Dotty shrugged. "I've never heard him, but I haven't seen him walking, not alone on a path such as this."

"What if they heard Enoch approaching at exactly the moment he heard them?" Mary mused.

"Or saw him through one of the gaps in those planks," Dotty added.

Mary nodded. "We're getting the picture of *how* this happened but still not *who*."

Dotty's downcast expression didn't lighten as they set out back to the Marmalades' house. She picked up a stick and swished it at every tall plant on the path side. That spoke of great perturbation, to Mary's mind.

"What is it, Dotty?"

"I envy plants," Dotty said. "Mating is so easy for them. They bloom, a bee comes by and brings pollen to them, and they have children. No fuss, no waiting, no misunderstandings, just as simple as a bee landing."

"You must be patient, my dear. Even plants have to wait for that bee to arrive."

"I don't have any appeal," Dotty replied, even more gloomily.

"Then you must get some."

"I'm not wearing all that cosmetic goo the others put on," Dotty asserted.

"Flowers have to bloom," Mary reminded her. "Sometimes it comes from within, sometimes it needs some help." *Dotty will shine before the year is out, or I'm not the Duchess of Snodsbury.*

BACK AT THE HOUSE, Dotty went off to find the others, and Mary, entering the drawing room, found Fran Beacham ranting to Nellie about police stupidity and overbearing arrogance. Mary's entrance stopped her mid-sentence.

"Oh, hello," Mary said. "You answered their questions successfully, then?"

"Yes," Fran said. "They found a safe in our house I didn't even know about. They wouldn't believe me. They think I'm a murderer! It took my lawyer to get me out of there."

"I'm sure Inspector Acton doesn't think you're the murderer," Nellie said soothingly.

Or you'd have been charged by now. Does this mean Nellie is the last suspect standing? Or is there another? Is it possible I was wrong about Cyril Beacham? Clear Nellie first, I think. Not me, though. It has to be Inspector Acton again.

22

NETTING THE CULPRIT

When Mary caught up with Cook in the kitchen and brought her away from the other servants, the sturdy woman was as unhappy about going back to question the other cooks as Dotty had been. "Milady, they'll throw me out if I keep badgering this way. It's never-ending."

"We'll soon have the answer to this riddle, Cook, and then we'll be gone. If we come back, it will all be forgotten. We'll be the heroes of this story."

Cook harrumphed, like an old man in a movie. "If you say so, milady, but I'm more concerned with the here and now, where I absolutely won't be a heroine but the nosy parker always ferreting out other people's private affairs."

"Their meal menus can hardly be considered 'private affairs,' Cook." Mary laughed.

Cook left to carry out her instructions but with the air of one going to the scaffold. Mary felt a twinge of guilt but rallied when she considered how she would feel when questioning the home-owners again about their meals. To be honest, she rather shared Cook's misgivings. But duty demanded it, and she began at once with Nellie and Gerry, who were adamant nothing involving smoked bacon or oysters had been on the menu in any of the days leading up to the murder. Satisfied, Mary with Barkley at her side, marched over to the Illingsworths' house to ask Victor Illingsworth.

He, however, was harder to tie down, his mind full of his wife's arrest and what the police might be doing to her.

"They won't be using physical violence, and you have your lawyer with her, so you needn't worry," Mary reminded him. "Now about the meals?"

"How should I know?" Victor said brusquely. "I don't remember things like that. Rose would know."

"But I can't ask Rose," Mary said patiently but through gritted teeth.

"Then ask our cook. She'll be in the kitchen, I imagine."

"You don't know?" Mary asked.

"Looking out for the servants is Rose's job," he replied.

Mary shook her head in dismay. *Men!*

"Whatever you like," Illingsworth said, dismissing her with a curt nod and returning to his newspaper.

The Illingsworths' cook didn't need to remember. The menu for the week was written out by Rose and kept in a cubby above the old-fashioned marble countertop. She handed it to Mary, who read it carefully. Nothing that suggested smoked bacon or oysters in any of the meals. She remarked on this to the cook.

"Mrs. Illingsworth doesn't like smoked bacon or oysters," the woman replied. "Mr. Illingsworth does—but he doesn't plan the menus."

Mary smiled. "He's in for a shock if Rose isn't out of custody by tomorrow night."

The cook frowned and crossed her arms. "I've tried to broach the subject with him, and he refuses to even consider the idea."

"He was the same with me just now," Mary said. "He's gone into a shell and won't come out."

The cook hesitated. "That would be on account of him knowing about his wife and Mr. Beacham but saying and doing nothing, I reckon."

"You're sure he knew?"

The cook nodded, her eyes widening. "He knew, all right."

"Then he may fear she's guilty of murder," Mary replied.

"Very likely he does," the woman said. "But she didn't poison Mr. Beacham with anything from here, for she left the house empty-handed that morning."

"What time was that?" Mary asked.

"I'm sure I've told your cook this before. It was about seven fifteen, and she had no breakfast because it wasn't ready until seven thirty."

"Do you know where she went?"

"She passed the kitchen window, so she was heading into the village. Going to the Beachams' house, I'd say."

"Rose told me she and Victor were together that morning," Mary said.

"Oh, she was back soon enough," the woman replied. "About eight, I'd say. Then they were together right up until leaving for the tennis tournament."

Mary thanked her for her help and wished Victor Illingsworth a pleasant day as she passed him, still staring at the newspaper but clearly not reading it. Outside, she decided she'd ask Fran if Rose had visited her that morning. Mary, with quick strides now that the evidence was piling up, walked to the Beachams' house.

Fran Beacham answered the door. Not the smartly dressed and groomed Fran Mary had seen before at the Marmalades' house. Her hair today was unkempt, she was still in her bathrobe, and her face was unadorned with makeup. The woman was certainly feeling the strain of the events swirling around her. Or was it something more? A guilty conscience, perhaps?

"Good morning, Fran." Mary smiled broadly in what she hoped was a disarming way that would gain her and Barkley entrance.

Fran stepped back, and Mary marched in before Fran could change her mind. "I hope you don't mind me coming here to ask more questions," Mary began.

Fran shook her head and offered Mary a seat.

Mary sat and, when Fran was seated opposite, said, "I'm wondering if you had any smoked bacon and oyster dishes in the days before Cyril's death."

"The police asked that," Fran said. "We didn't on those days, but we often did. Cyril loved *Angels on Horseback*. He said they kept him virile."

"It's a common belief among men, I understand," Mary said. "The oysters, I mean."

Fran snorted in contempt.

"Your cook couldn't have made up a batch just for him?" Mary asked, grasping at straws.

"She could, I suppose," Fran said. "She often made him things he liked for snacks."

Mary laughed. "She thought a lot of Cyril, then?"

Fran smiled sadly. "Cyril had an appetite for all the good things in life. I, sadly, have to diet. I think the cook liked having someone who appreciated her cooking. A satisfied customer must be a blessing to someone who works every day, providing meals with never a word or gesture of appreciation."

Mary considered this and blushed. "You've just made me feel bad. I don't believe I've ever truly told my cook how much I appreciate her."

Fran made eye contact with Mary. "You see things differently when something like this happens. Janet's devastated by Cyril's death, and I can't help feeling it's because he appreciated her. Cyril could make any woman feel better about themselves."

"I had the impression," Mary said slowly, "some women didn't appreciate his manner."

"You mean Nellie?" Fran said. "It's true. Nellie's a very old-fashioned woman when it comes to social settings, and Cyril was very cosmopolitan in his manners. 'I have too much London polish for Nellie,' he'd say, and laugh."

"Do you think your cook would talk to me about bacon and oysters?" Mary asked.

"I'll call her in, and we'll see," Fran said. "She might be more comfortable if I'm here." She left the room and, after a brief conversation Mary couldn't quite hear, returned with a short, middle-aged, yet voluptuous woman, who looked exactly like anyone would imagine a cook to look.

"Hello." Mary smiled. "I'm Lady Mary Culpeper. I'm staying at the Marmalades' and trying to make sense of what happened to poor Cyril."

The woman silently nodded, leaving Fran to introduce her. "Janet Harbottle, Lady Mary," Fran said. "Janet has been our cook for as long as I've been here."

Barkley trotted across the floor to sniff at the hem of the cook's long dress and apron until Mary called him back. He returned, making strange low growling sounds before settling at Mary's feet.

Miss Harbottle ignored Barkley. "I know who you are and what you're doing."

There was an admirable stolid vigor in her answer that was at odds with the gentle handling Fran had suggested she might need. If either of the two needed support from the other, it was Fran from the cook.

"You'll also know the police think he was poisoned by

smoked bacon and oysters, which I understand from Mrs. Beacham was something of a favorite of Mr. Beacham's."

"No secret in that. Mr. Beacham liked *angels on horseback*, and I would make them for him, when he asked."

"Did he ask that morning?"

The woman shook her head. "He was out of the house before breakfast was made that day."

"Did you see him leave?"

"No, but I heard him, or at least I assumed it was him. I was in the pantry, and there's no window."

"You then made breakfast, assuming he would return and eat it?"

"That's right. I prepared the meal and put it on top of the stove to keep warm. Mrs. Beacham likes to lie in, and I didn't want the food cold when Mr. Beacham returned."

"Then you did what?"

The cook frowned. "I'm afraid I put my feet up and rested. I didn't see any harm in it. I have all day to wash up."

"You were alone?"

"I'm the only live-in servant, and Sunday was Edie's day off. She's the maid here."

"Did you hear Mrs. Beacham go out?"

"I didn't. I'm ashamed to say, I'd fallen asleep by then."

"You didn't leave the house at all?" Mary found this hard to believe.

"No, madam, I didn't."

"We were told a man who may have been Mr. Beacham's partner was knocking on the door that morning," Mary said, trying to gauge from the cook's face if she was surprised by this.

"Good heavens," Harbottle said. "I must have been out like a light. Though it can be hard to hear the front doorbell from my room when the hall door is closed."

"The person who told us this was speaking of the back door," Mary said.

"Ah. Then I definitely wouldn't have heard it. The back door joins a small corridor that has two doors before it opens up to the house and hall. You can't hear anyone that would be there, unless you're actually in the kitchen or pantry."

"Well," Mary said, "thank you for your help. Bit by bit, I'm getting a picture of what happened in the village that morning and where everyone was."

The cook smiled and left with the same vigorous stride and posture she'd had throughout the interview. If anyone could have murdered anyone in Upper Wainbury, Beacham's cook would be Mary's first guess. But, a middle-aged woman with graying hair and a grim expression was hardly Cyril Beacham's type. And his fastidious artistic persona wouldn't have allowed him to have an affair with a cook; Mary was sure of that.

"Fran," Mary said when the cook was out of hearing. "Where did you go that morning?"

"I thought I'd told you this. I went for a walk."

"But where?"

"Along the lane, past the train station," Fran replied. "There's a crabapple tree down that way, and I pick its fruit every year for jelly, when they're ripe. It's too early now but I keep checking it on my walks."

"And you didn't see your husband?"

"No, I didn't."

"Was anything missing when you returned home that morning?" Mary asked. "I'm thinking of the man at the door and peering through the window."

"Nothing of mine," Fran said. "I didn't know about the man, so I haven't looked at Cyril's things."

"Please look today," Mary begged. "It could be important."

"How?" Fran asked. "Even if someone stole something that belonged to Cyril, this isn't where he died."

"I know, but the man could have known where he'd find Cyril. Maybe they'd arranged to meet somewhere, so he took the opportunity of Cyril being out to burgle the house."

"But he would assume the servants and I would be in," Fran objected.

"Maybe he knew you only have one live-in servant, and he hoped he could gain admittance by knocking on the door, explaining who he was, and saying he'd wait until Cyril returned."

Fran flashed a look of contemplation. "All right, I'll look, but if he took something like business correspondence, I won't know. However, you should know, the police took most of Cyril's papers on the day he died."

"Thanks, Fran, just do your best with what's still here," Mary said. "I'll get out of your way and let you dress. Phone me if you do find something missing. That man must have wanted something." She rose from her chair after ruffing her corgi's fur to alert him that they were leaving, and allowed Fran to escort them to the door.

Mary returned to the Marmalade house, contemplating Fran and her whole demeanor this morning. *Which suggested guilt, but was it? Knowing her husband liked* angels on horseback, *could she have made up a batch, followed him and carried out the murder? But why would they go to a country farmer's shed when they had a nice snug bed and home of their own? Was it because the cook lived in and they were enjoying some sexual pleasures they didn't want her to hear? That cry Enoch had heard, and the odd assortment of clothes and other items, suggested it might be so. And Fran had a much better motive than Rose Illingsworth.*

And what was it about Janet Harbottle that had sparked some hint in Mary's mind? Something in her appearance was disquiet-

ing, only Mary couldn't put her finger on it. *The woman looked well, very well; none of that pasty look so many cooks had from living indoors. Janet Harbottle was blooming, her skin radiant.* Her resolute character was also a surprise. Domestics were usually ill at ease in the presence of people they considered their superiors; Miss Harbottle was not. It was a puzzle she'd sleep on, and the answer would come to her as it always did.

"Barkley," Mary said to her companion. "It's all very unsatisfactory."

She was good at reading Barkley's expressions, and right now she would guess he was suggesting that he'd found the clue and provided the answer. As so often happened, Mary wished she could have smelled what he'd smelled.

Mary arrived back at the Marmalade house in time for lunch and a barrage of questions from her assistants and Nellie.

"What did you learn at the Beachams'?"

"The most interesting thing I learned is the Beachams' cook, Miss Harbottle, says Cyril went out, and believing Fran to be still in bed, she put up her feet to rest and fell asleep."

"That isn't much of a clue," Winnie replied. "She was late here that day because she fell asleep?"

"It means she doesn't have an alibi, stoopid," Dotty retorted.

"Was that it?" Margie asked. "All that time and that's all you got?"

"Didn't Dotty tell you? Barkley found a clue, which I'm taking to Inspector Acton after lunch," Mary replied. "Beyond that, I rather agree with you. I'm not sure we're any further forward. In fact, I think we may be on the wrong path altogether."

Winnie and Dotty promptly demanded to go with her to the police station, and she obliged. Margie said she had things to do and wouldn't join them on this expedition.

"Ponsonby will be on the two-thirty train," Mary replied to

Margie. "If you're in the village, you might accompany him on the walk here from the station. See he doesn't get lost." She laughed.

Margie flushed pink but agreed she might be able to do that, if her errands were done by then.

23

DROP SHOT

Inspector Acton examined the plastic sword and attached pieces of flesh with distaste. "And you say you found this near the shed?"

"Barkley found it in the hedge, only yards away," Mary replied. "I hoped your lab could confirm it has a sedative in the meat and which it is. You can't get strong sedatives without a prescription, so it should identify our murderer."

Acton nodded. "Unless it's so common every woman in the village uses it."

"There is that chance."

"There's so little left to analyze, I fear it may not be possible," Acton added. "Still, they can try."

"The birds and animals have eaten most of the meat," Mary agreed. "But to knock out a man of Beacham's size would require a hefty dose. I think there's a strong likelihood your lab will find something."

As Acton escorted them out of the police station, he said, "By the way, we're following up on your information about Beacham, his partner and their associates. With the papers we took from Beacham's study, the boys in London are quite excited. I think Mr. Marmalade might get the justice he's longed for all these years, after all."

"I hope so, Inspector. And if I may, I'd like to suggest letting Rose Illingsworth go at this time. I've never heard of her needing strong sedatives."

"Mrs. Beacham is the most likely of the three," Acton confirmed. "We're letting Mrs. Illingsworth go home today."

"Dotty," Mary said. "Here's the car key. You two go ahead. I want a word with the Inspector."

The girls looked mutinous but headed for the car. When they were out of earshot, Mary turned to Acton, hesitated, and drew a deep breath. "I have another possible avenue to explore."

"We have many avenues we haven't yet explored," Acton said. "Which one is this?"

"Again, I implore you not to mention I told you this," Mary said. "If I'm wrong, I still want to be friends with the Marmalades."

"Is it Mrs. Marmalade this time? You were wrong about Mr. Marmalade, you know. I'm not sure I see his wife being the killer either."

"Nellie told me she was supervising the staff all that morning before the other guests arrived," Mary said. "Their cook says she never saw Nellie at all that morning. It's not much to go on, but I'm letting you know. It's up to you what you do with it."

"You think she was one of Beacham's girlfriends?"

"She was very quick to tell me early on that people might think she was having an affair with Mr. Illingsworth. Rose Illingsworth thinks it was with Beacham."

"What do your helpers know about Mrs. Marmalade's movements that morning?"

"I haven't asked them because they would guess I suspect Nellie," Mary replied.

"Do you?"

Mary hesitated. "Yes. I do. I have doubts, but I'm fairly certain she's hiding something, and if it isn't murdering Beacham, it's probably an affair with him."

"How do you think she poisoned him?"

"We've assumed the meal was cooked in a local kitchen, but there are ready-made meals in high-end London shops these days. Probably Bristol also. You just heat and serve. No mess, no fuss, and little smell. The actual poisoning is easy to explain. Nellie was a nurse helper in the war; she knows her way around a hypodermic."

"I'll have her brought in for questioning and the house and grounds searched again," Acton said. "I hope you're right this time, or Mr. Marmalade and I will be enemies for years to come. I may never win another case when he's presiding."

"I understand. I feel it too." Mary paused. "You *will* let me know if the lab finds anything?"

Acton appeared to consider, then grinned. "If they find nothing, I'll let you know right away. If they find something we can use, and our investigation finds the person it was prescribed to, I'll let you know right *after* we have them in custody." He headed back to the station.

Mary walked back to the car. The moment she was in, Dotty said, "You have an idea who it is, don't you?"

"Yes, I think I do, but I can't say anything until we hear back from the inspector, and then it will be too late to appear a genius."

LATER THAT DAY, after most of the household had gone to bed, the phone rang. Mary, who was in her room, grabbed the handset quickly so no one else could take the call.

"Yes?" she whispered.

"Your Grace," Acton replied. "I have good news and bad news."

"Tell me the bad news first," Mary said.

"I phoned Mrs. Marmalade and asked her about that morning. She had thought she felt a migraine coming on and had been resting on her bed with a cold flannel on her forehead. The maid has confirmed it. Mrs. Marmalade didn't want the party spoiled and had asked the maid to keep quiet. We won't be arresting her."

"But you will continue investigating," Mary said.

"No, because I have good news."

Mary listened, and a wave of relief swept over her. There'd be no fight with Nellie or Gerry, no lost friendship, and Margie would still be one of the Society of Six. However, her earlier decision to never investigate her friends would stand. In all her cases, she'd been sure this or that person was the culprit, and when she had been wrong, it meant nothing to her. She'd squeaked through this one because Acton had kept her secret. For the future, she must remember the people she pointed a finger at were people, real people with families and feelings. Her choices in this case had been painful to make, and they were wrong. It must never happen again.

THE FOLLOWING MORNING, triumphant assistants, unusually relaxed Cook, excited Barkley, and the always self-controlled Ponsonby, gathered around Lady Mary as she responded to Nellie's demand to be told how the team had solved the mystery.

"Well," Mary said, "we mustn't forget that without the police services, we wouldn't have done so."

"But without you and the others' persistence," Gerry said before puffing on his pipe, "they would still be plodding on and quite possibly never have found it, or worse, charged poor Rose here"—he gestured to Rose Illingsworth, who still looked shaken by her ordeal—"and she could have been wrongly convicted."

"I don't know where to start," Mary said.

"At the beginning," Dotty replied matter-of-factly. "With the odd happenings."

"Yes, we should get them out of the way first," Mary suggested. "You'll remember, I hope, those incidents are what the girls initially suspected would point to a possible crime, likely murder."

The assembled group of the Marmalades, the Illingsworths, and Fran Beacham nodded impatiently.

"They were explained away as being unconnected, and most were, but not the two killings," Mary said. "Ponsonby described them as being in three categories. First, the puncture, and that has a simple common explanation. Second, the car failures, and they were because of poor maintenance, one specifically by an elderly man working long past his prime. And lastly, most significantly, the two animal deaths."

Mary saw, with some amusement, her listeners' frustration was growing more apparent. She continued, "The first two categories, as I've said, were unconnected. The third one, however, was real and the girls' feeling that these deaths were someone practicing, was absolutely right."

"Of course we were," Margie said. "It was obvious."

"But among all the other incidents, they were lost to view. Just two old pets that died." Mary smiled.

"You're saying that woman deliberately killed those animals to get the dose right for a man?" Nellie asked.

"Oh yes," Mary said. "Remember, she's a cook. To get the

recipe right, you need the right amounts of ingredients. This was a recipe she'd never made before, and she wanted it to be right on the day."

"But when did you suspect it was her?" Fran Beacham asked.

"About halfway through our search, but I couldn't believe it," Mary said. "I was convinced I understood the character of Cyril, and he and she couldn't be the answer. People are often surprising."

"It staggers me," Gerry said. "Beacham and his cook, Miss Harbottle—never in a million years, I'd have said."

"We all figured it was his artistic nature that accounted for the women he chose," Mary said. "And assumed it was the only thing that drove his desires."

"I knew there was someone," Rose Illingsworth muttered. "I even told you, remember?"

"That's when I began to suspect we didn't know Cyril as well as we thought." Mary nodded. "But I still couldn't quite believe it."

"What clinched it?" Victor Illingsworth asked.

"Barkley's discovery." Mary patted his head as he rushed to her side at the sound of his name. "The police lab said the remaining fragments of oyster had been packaged in oil. The fishmonger, of course, sells only fresh oysters. Just one house bought a can of oysters in oil from the village store, and that was the Beachams."

"I had no idea," Fran Beacham said.

"Nor would you need to," Mary replied. "Your cook did the grocery shopping."

"And they identified the sedative," Dotty blurted. She'd had a hand in this part.

Mary smiled at Dotty's excitement. "It's true, I knew there was a strong likelihood the lab would find something. Even though there was very little of the *angel on horseback* left, there was so much sedative in the meat, it was still showing up a week later, and they found it."

"It's called Distaval or Thalidomide, and it's brand new on the market," Dotty said breathlessly. "It treats the side effects of pregnancy, but it sends you to sleep as well."

"Only one doctor has prescribed it in this area," Mary said. "And he prescribed it to Miss Harbottle, who, as you might have guessed from what's just been said, is pregnant with Beacham's child."

"What?" Nellie cried, "He wouldn't, she wouldn't."

"Then why would she kill her child's father?" Gerry demanded, incredulous at Mary's bold assertion.

"Because he wouldn't marry her," Mary replied. "He'd promised to do so, and kept her thinking he would, but then, just a day or so before, he told her he wasn't divorcing Fran."

"The shame would be too much for her, I would think," Nellie's gaze lowered and her voice softened. "Poor woman."

"You'd think," Dotty said thoughtfully, "Beacham would've been pleased to have a child because he and Fran haven't any."

"That may have been a choice," Mary waved her hand. "And finding Miss Harbottle was pregnant was what changed his mind about marrying her. He just didn't want children."

"I still find it amazing," Gerry flashed a puzzled look. "I can't imagine Beacham finding Miss Harbottle attractive."

"They had common interests..." Mary replied. "Food ... and ... I haven't one of those other odd passions, so I can't fully understand it myself. All I can say is, when two people discover they share such a passion, the attraction seems to be mutual and takes no account of appearance or status."

"Apparently not," Gerry dismissed. "I know I'm a bit conventional in these matters, so I'll have to accept your explanation, Mary. I just can't truly believe it."

"You don't have passions, Gerry," Nellie scoffed. "So how could you understand?"

Gerry's face reddened and he set his pipe down before moving for the door. "Quite right, my dear," he acquiesced.

There was an uncomfortable silence before Winnie asked, "Didn't Enoch Cutler help you as well?"

Grateful for the change of subject, Mary said, "He did. Thank you for reminding me, Winnie."

"I wouldn't believe much of what that young tearaway told you," Nellie objected.

"In this case his evidence was almost certainly correct. He heard a woman cry out as he was near the shed where Beacham met with Janet Harbottle."

"Did he recognize the voice?" Victor Illingsworth asked.

Mary shook her head. "He says not, and I imagine it would be hard to do so from a single cry. What he did say was that the cry wasn't like someone in distress."

Ponsonby added, "From the garments and implements we saw in our search, I'd say the cry was definitely not from distress."

"No indeed," Mary replied. "Quite the opposite, but, like Gerry, that isn't something I can properly understand."

Gerry nodded. "I find that kind of thing completely incomprehensible, as I'm sure most of us do."

There was a general murmur of agreement that Mary found unconvincing, but she couldn't quite say why.

"I think it would be the smell of cooking I'd find unattractive," Victor Illingsworth said. "You know what I mean, that smell that comes from always working with vegetables and raw meat. It must be hard to lose, even on off days, which Harbottle never took, so far as I could see."

Fran Beacham nodded. "That's true, she didn't. She said she

had no family or friends to visit, so she stayed in our house. She never even took a holiday."

"That may have been to stay near Cyril," Mary said.

"Oh no," Fran said. "That is her way—from the day she arrived. I don't believe their affair has gone on long. I would've known. I always do, eventually." Her gaze settled on Rose Illingsworth, who glanced away.

"Well," Rose said, "I hope that explains our part in this sorry affair."

"But it doesn't cover everything," Gerry said. "What about the blackmail letters? And that man Winkler hanging around Fran's house?"

"For an explanation of those, we do have to wait for the police to get here," Mary said. "They promised to be here today, and they're late."

"But you and Ponsonby learned things in London," Rose Illingsworth said. "And the girls found out things here too. You must be able to say something about them?"

"My hardworking assistants did indeed learn a lot about all those sides of the story," Mary agreed. "And we handed over what we learned to the police. They have used the information well, and I understand arrests have been made in London."

"And you think Inspector Acton will share that with us?" Victor asked bitterly.

"He said he would," Mary replied. "And I think he's a man of his word."

"Maybe we should have some tea and scones while we wait." Nellie rang the bell for the maid, who appeared almost instantly.

"Tell the cook we need tea, scones and cakes, Lizzy," Nellie said. The maid hurried off to deliver the message, leaving the group silently considering all they'd heard.

Mary watched the expressions and noted, fearfully, Gerry's gaze at Nellie. It didn't bode well for the future. Nellie's gibe about his "lack of passions" so publicly expressed, had struck a nerve.

"I hope the cakes arrive before Inspector Acton does," Margie said. "I'm starving. The excitement of investigating and the eventual successful conclusion makes me hungry."

"You'll want to celebrate, I expect," Winnie added.

"I won't celebrate if she's hanged," Dotty interjected. "I don't believe in killing people."

24

CHAMPIONSHIP CLUE

Winnie's hopes were fulfilled because it was almost an hour before Inspector Acton and Sergeant Reynolds arrived, and the scones and cakes were gone by then.

"We had some loose ends being tied up in London," Acton replied, when Mary asked what had kept them. "They're finished now, so I can tell you of our successful conclusion to this case."

Our success. "What can you tell us from your side of the case, Inspector?"

"Well, first, Janet Harbottle has confessed to murdering Cyril Beacham and will be duly prosecuted." Acton leaned his elbow against the mantelpiece.

"And her reason for the heinous act?" Mary asked.

"As you'd suspected, Lady Mary. She was carrying the victim's child, and he'd refused to acknowledge it, or her. She's a woman of strong traditional beliefs, and in her mind, his betrayal warranted her response. She has no remorse, and this will be a problem for her defense."

"But what about the crooked business deals?" Gerry asked tersely.

"Fortunately for us we'd removed all the victim's papers from his home office before his business partner could get hold of them, though he'd tried some weeks earlier, before the burglary and before the murder."

"Why couldn't he get them?" Victor Illingsworth asked. "There was no one at the Beachams' house that night, as I recall."

"Ah, yes," Acton said. "Mr. and Mrs. Beacham weren't home, that's true, but Janet Harbottle *was*, and she scared him off. She didn't know him and thought it was a burglary. She's a formidable woman. I'm not surprised he ran off."

"And the next time?" Victor pressed.

"He got in when no one was at home," Acton replied. "But he couldn't find the paperwork about the phony artwork they'd sold."

"Does phony artwork need papers?" Rose Illingsworth asked.

"Of course," Acton replied. "If they're to convince a buyer the piece is real, it has to have all the right provenance."

"But you found the proof *you* needed?" Mary asked.

"We did. It was cunningly hidden in a safe behind a secret door cut into the old wainscoting. Mr. Winkler's two attempts to get the paperwork clued us in that there was something there, and we found it."

Fran Beacham scoffed, most unladylike. "You wouldn't believe me when I said I didn't know about his business."

"Mrs. Beacham, that you didn't know anything about a safe that took several days to install in a house you've lived in for eight years wasn't a very convincing story." He frowned. "It still isn't, in my mind."

"I've told you," Fran cried angrily. "Cyril lived in the house years before we married, and I never saw him go to that safe. And he kept his business dealings very private."

"Understandably, Mrs. Beacham. As it turns out, there doesn't seem to be a dodgy antique or art scheme they haven't done," he added.

"Have you arrested him?" Ponsonby asked.

"Mr. Winkler?"

"Yes."

"We have, and a sorrier-looking crook I've never met," Acton replied. "He wants us to believe everything was Mr. Beacham's idea, and his doing also."

"Are you convinced?" Mary asked.

Acton, grinning, shook his head. "No, and I don't think a jury will be either."

"He won't appear trustworthy to any juror," Ponsonby said. "I can't imagine how the gallery has kept going with him as its face."

"He had a much more personable salesman," Acton said. "Winkler generally kept to the shadows."

"If they were crooks," Mary said, "others must also have been involved, otherwise they'd never get away with it."

Acton nodded. "The Art Squad are rounding up plenty of others as we speak. They're very pleased with the information we provided."

"Will we get a medal?" Dotty asked.

Acton laughed. "Unlikely. I'm sorry."

"I've a question," Gerry spurted. "What about those letters? Who sent them? And why did I get them as well?"

"That's an interesting story," Acton noted. "And one I'll leave others to tell." His gaze turned to Victor Illingsworth.

"All right," Victor said, embarrassed. "I did send the letters, but not for money."

Gerry hissed at this revelation.

Acton moved to the center of the room. "Which is why you aren't being charged with a crime."

"I wanted him to leave the village, that's all," Victor said. "If Cyril left, Rose would be herself again. At least, that's what I thought."

"But how did you know about this?" Gerry said through gritted teeth. "And why send letters to me?"

Victor's expression was apologetic. "It was a chance encounter. I was in London some years ago on business. I had time to kill, and it was raining. A hall was holding an antique sales event, near my hotel. I don't have an interest in antiques, but it seemed like a good way to spend an hour." He shrugged. "I was talking to one dealer when I saw Beacham at a stall on the other side of the room. I mentioned to the dealer that Beacham lived in my village, and the guy frowned and shook his head."

"It didn't take much cajoling. He told me a story about art looting in Berlin in 1945," Victor continued. "He was there at the time and knew exactly what was going on. He said Beacham got away with it because of people higher up the chain and the incompetent investigation held."

Gerry flushed. "That's not true. We explored every avenue available to us," he shouted, and Acton stepped closer.

"I didn't know who led the investigation, Gerry, but then the man told me the name of the officer in charge—you!" Victor pointed.

"He had no right telling a complete stranger any of this," Gerry argued. "It's slanderous."

"I asked him what proof he had," Victor continued. "He said he'd been there, and that was proof enough. He said I should have nothing to do with Beacham."

"You said nothing at the time?" Mary asked.

Victor shook his head. "Even when Rose began her infatuation with Beacham, I didn't want to say what I knew, and I thought the letters were a good way of scaring him away."

"Why those cryptic letters to me?" Gerry demanded.

"When I found Beacham wasn't doing what I wanted, I thought you could hurry him along if I wrote you letters that looked like they came from Beacham. You would confront him, and he might finally get the message."

"And *my* feelings on the matter? What about those?"

"You were a soldier," Victor retorted. "Why would I assume your feelings might be hurt?"

"Leave it, Gerry." Nellie put a hand on his shoulder.

"That's good advice, Mr. Marmalade," Acton said. "Because you'll want to hear what I have to say."

Silence filled the room, and all eyes darted to Acton.

"During our interviews with Mr. Illingsworth, he provided us with the name of the dealer who'd warned him away from Beacham. The police in London interviewed the man, and now there's a case to be made about that crime."

"What?" Gerry cried.

"If it does come to court," Acton said, "you'll be required as a witness."

"But Beacham's dead?" Mary said.

"There were others who made out like bandits," Acton said. "Everyone believed Beacham the perpetrator, but there were others who walked away with thousands in stolen goods, and *they're* still very much alive."

"I'll be happy to be a witness if it will finally clear my name," Gerry said. "I've lived with this hanging over me too long. I just want to be free of it."

"Do you remember the army officers in charge then?" Acton asked.

"Their names are seared on my brain. I can never forget, or forgive."

"You weren't given the support you should've had," Sergeant Reynolds said, breaking his silence.

"No. But to be fair, at the time, I didn't seriously consider they were in on it," Gerry replied. "I just thought they were placing too much emphasis on the regiment's good name."

"You won't have kept in touch with them, then?" Reynolds asked.

"Certainly not," Gerry said. "Their behavior toward me at the end was unforgivable. My fellow investigator at the time, Major Lennox, will say the same, I'm sure."

"Sergeant Reynolds has been given the task of gathering information from witnesses outside London," Acton said. "Perhaps, before we leave, you and he can arrange an interview to record what you know and who you know so their evidence can be added."

Gerry nodded, his expression grim but satisfied.

"We have to leave now," Acton said. "But I do want to thank Lady Mary and her team for all the assistance. And to those here today who were witnesses and suspects, I understand how you must feel. Investigating a crime like murder is never easy on people, whether you're the interrogator or the interrogatee."

With that, Inspector Acton left the room, and Sergeant Reynolds took Gerry aside to organize the interview.

"Well," Mary said, smiling, "it's nice to be thanked for our efforts."

"Our efforts!" Margie cried. "*We* solved the case and handed it to him on a plate!"

Mary laughed. "I share your feelings, Margie, but the truth is, the police investigate crimes, and they do so with information given to them by the public. Strictly speaking, Inspector Acton's statement was correct."

"After all, we can't gather the evidence and make the case," Dotty said. "But I also feel we received faint praise which is better than none."

"I'm just happy it's over and Gerry might now get the dark cloud lifted from him. He deserves it." Nellie looked anxiously at her husband, who was still in earnest conversation with Sergeant Reynolds.

"I hope it will be too," Mary said. "But you both shouldn't expect too much from this. No one will know he's been exonerated of incompetence and being implicated in what happened—it's all so long ago, and everyone is scattered."

"You're probably right," Nellie said. "But Gerry will know, and his two friends, Lennox and Foreman, will too. They'll feel easier knowing the truth."

Mary was tempted to say "the truth" was an elusive thing that rarely appeared when governments were involved, but she didn't. Nellie and Gerry needed all the good news they could get after these past days.

"And you, Fran," Nellie asked, perhaps sensing Mary's doubts, "what will you do now?"

"I'm not sure. I imagine the London gallery will be closed. No one will buy anything there once the trial of Winkler's and Cyril's associates begins, so I'll get nothing from that. That leaves me this house and some art and antique pieces to sell, if they truly belong to the business."

"Will you stay in Upper Wainbury?" Mary asked.

"I think not," Fran replied. "Too much has happened for it to be comfortable."

"But none of it was your fault," Rose cried.

"No," Fran said. "Though, as Gerry discovered all those years ago, people don't trust people who they feel must have known, or even been part of, the events. I'll start again somewhere where none of this will have been heard of. What about you two?" Fran peered at Victor and Rose.

The couple glanced at each other, deciding who should speak. Victor replied, "We haven't decided yet. As you said, Fran, people will always look at us differently because we were both held for some time by the police. 'There's no smoke without fire' is what they'll think, even if they never say it."

Gerry, who'd rejoined them as Victor was speaking, said, "I understand how you feel. I mean, who will come to a tennis or any other kind of party at our house after this?"

"But, Papa," Margie said, "he wasn't poisoned at the party. He only died here."

Her father smiled sadly. "I'm afraid it doesn't work that way, my dear. We"—he gestured to the Illingsworths, Fran Beacham, and Nellie—"are all tarnished by what happened. It will be thought the way we all behaved caused the murder to happen."

"You don't want to leave, do you?" Margie asked anxiously.

"I don't, but we shall see how this unfolds," Gerry replied. "If we're snubbed by our neighbors, or not invited to local events, and if my position in the community is lost, then we may have to leave."

"But we helped find the murderer and bring those looters to justice," Margie said. "That must count for something."

Her father crossed the floor and opened his arms. "As I said, my dear, we must wait and see."

"It's so unfair," Margie complained. "Why should we have to move away because an unpleasant man died in our garden?"

Her father wrapped his little girl in a big hug. "Life isn't fair, believe me. Sometimes, though, it all comes right in the end. Maybe it will for us this time."

THE VISITORS and the inspectors had left, Nellie and Gerry had gone out for a walk and, Mary suspected, a serious discussion of their future, so Mary and Ponsonby took Barkley for his exercise. They were careful to go the opposite way as the Marmalades.

As they passed the shed where the poisoning had taken place, Ponsonby said, "Mrs. Beacham may get something from the furnishings there." He gestured to the shed.

"I hope so," Mary said. "I don't know if she has any income of her own."

"We were told she has money," Ponsonby said.

"She certainly didn't sound like she could live on it when she was speaking earlier."

"It's possible she covered too many gaps in the gallery's income and her funds are low," Ponsonby agreed.

"If the looking glass in the shed is real and not a fake, I think it may be worth a tidy sum," Mary said. "I don't know about the other pieces."

"They looked old," Ponsonby said. "Whether they're genuine antiques or not, only a dealer can say. We should remove the garments and other items, my lady, before Mrs. Beacham sees them."

Mary smiled. Trust Ponsonby to imagine a woman like Fran Beacham would be horrified by such things. "Strictly speaking, they belong to her as well," Mary reminded him.

"If you think it wise, my lady," Ponsonby said. "I still feel it would be a kindness to remove them."

"Here's Enoch striding up the path like a man on a mission." Mary pointed to the figure climbing steadily toward them.

"Miss Marmalade did say she was going out this afternoon," Ponsonby replied cryptically.

"Winnie and Dotty won't be pleased to be left alone." Mary frowned. "Perhaps we should return and entertain them."

"I believe they're all going to the county fair, my lady," Ponsonby said. "I'm sure they'll find enough friends there."

Mary laughed. "It won't only be Nellie who's upset if the girls all want to marry farmers."

"The young ladies will do what's best for them," Ponsonby said, evenly.

Enoch passed them with a beaming smile and a loud "Good day" without breaking his stride. They watched him for a moment and returned to their walk. "Oh, to be young again." Mary sighed.

25

TENNIS COURT CONCLUSIONS

GERRY

In the few days that followed, and before Mary left, life for the people involved began to return to normal. They supported each other with mutual invitations to visit, and the girls played tennis until they dropped into their beds each night from exhaustion.

Gerry's worst fears about being snubbed or losing his positions didn't happen. Whether it was because he and the others were now considered witnesses, and therefore interesting, and not suspects nor dangerous, wasn't clear. Whatever it was, the Conservative Club didn't throw him out, and he was back on the bench, providing justice to the usual local poachers, litterers, and people accused of other assorted misdemeanors.

Even the Illingsworths found they were considered desirable guests who could recount interesting tales of police interrogations and cold cells. They too began to relax and gently fall back into the bosom of the community.

Fran Beacham, however, was cast out for being too closely connected to the villains, for Cyril too was now seen to be a criminal, which, of course, everyone said they'd known all along.

"My dear," Nellie said one evening to Gerry as they prepared for bed, "we asked Mary to visit during our tennis tournament, which never concluded. Don't you think we should hold it now, as Mary is leaving Monday?"

"Are you sure, Nellie?" Gerry asked.

"I've talked to the Illingsworths, and they will come," Nellie replied. "And the vicar will come too, with Mrs. Alderson as a partner. You'll have to keep Mr. Alderson entertained." Mr. Alderson had one leg shorter than the other after a war injury, and all sports but golf were beyond him.

"And Fran?" Gerry asked.

"She doesn't feel up to it," Nellie said. "Understandably, I suppose."

"Quite," Gerry replied.

"I've sounded out those who made last year's tournament so exciting," Nellie said nonchalantly.

"You feel their antics might erase the memory of what happened," Gerry said.

"Perhaps mixed bathing naked in our pool isn't the worst thing that can happen at a party."

"Quite," Gerry replied. "Well, you have it well in hand. We can't call it off now."

"Quite," said Nellie, with a sly smile only her mirror saw.

MARY

THE TENNIS TOURNAMENT was a great success. Even Mary played one game with Ponsonby as her partner. They had an amazing run of good fortune and won the game. Their good fortune disappeared in the next round against a young couple who weren't better tennis players but infinitely stronger and faster. Mary's assistant sleuths, aided by the sporty Vanessa, trounced everyone now that the ever-competitive Cyril Beacham was gone.

"You have to let youngsters win." Victor sipped his Pimms, watching the girls splashing in the pool to celebrate their victory.

"Exactly my feelings," Gerry said through a puff on his pipe. "Youth must have its fling, right?"

Mary laughed. "This is the most satisfying ending to my visit, Nellie. I'm glad it has turned out so well for you."

"Oh, yes," the vicar, who was hard of hearing, said. "The weather has been glorious. We get so few days like this, this late in the season."

"Is there anything I can get you, my lady?" Ponsonby asked, hovering nearby.

"Nothing, thank you, Ponsonby."

"Then I shall go and join the servants, who have invited Cook and me to join them in their own celebration. I suspect to show no hard feelings about the events of the past week."

"Then by all means go." Mary grinned. "Just be sure we're ready to travel in the morning."

"My lady! There will be no question of anything of that nature, I assure you."

Mary laughed and returned her attention to the pool, where a group of young men had appeared from nowhere. Her smile grew even broader as she considered what the vicar might say if events similar to the previous year's transpired.

EPILOGUE

The sun hung low in the sky, casting a warm golden hue over the rolling hills of the English countryside. Her Grace, Mary, Duchess of Snodsbury, leaned back in the plush seat of her Rolls Royce, the breeze threatening to tousle her beehive bun. The young sleuths had made sure Mary looked her finest for her departure. Sitting beside her, Barkley surveyed the passing scenery with an air of dignified curiosity, his nose pressed to the closed window on their side, in a most undignified way.

The rhythmic hum of the engine and the gentle purr of the wind were soothing. Her eyes wandered over the fields, her mind momentarily free from the responsibilities of crime solving and being a duchess. In front of her, Ponsonby was navigating with his driving face on, and Cook, seated to his right, was chattering about their final weekend and the fair, which she'd attended with the Marmalade house staff.

"Did the fair compare with the one we have in the village at Snodsbury every year?" Mary asked Cook.

She turned to face Mary, her expression one of astonishment. "Nothing can compare to our local fair, milady. Still," she continued, "it had rides and sideshows. I do love the distorting mirrors, they're such a laugh."

Mary guffawed. "Once, I would have agreed," she said. "Today, I fear I'd cry to see myself in them."

Ponsonby added, "I always enjoyed the dodgems, when I was young."

Rounding a bend in the road, a jolt bounced the three of them as the car hit a rough patch.

"Sorry, ma'am." Ponsonby flicked a glance to his rearview mirror.

The car jostled, leaned, and then started grinding along the pavement. Ponsonby slowed to a stop as he pulled to the side of the road. "Looks like we have a flat, my lady."

Lady Mary sighed. With a hint of amusement, she said, "Ah, the joys of the open road, Ponsonby."

Ponsonby parked the car and killed the engine. Mary opened her door. Stepping out onto the grassy verge, she stretched her limbs, relishing the sensation after being confined to the car for over an hour.

Barkley hopped out behind her, his ears perked as he sniffed the unfamiliar scents of the countryside. Mary bent to scratch his back, her thoughts turning to the grand renovation project underway at Snodsbury estate. "I do hope the new rose garden will be ready by the time we return," Mary mused. "It's been years since we've been in such a fine state."

Ponsonby emerged from the car's boot with a spare tire and the necessary tools. He removed his jacket and rolled up his sleeves. "Indeed. The garden's transformation will be quite the spectacle. The roses, the fountains, and the new pergola—all coming together to create a splendid sight, I'm sure."

Cook, with her rotund frame and good-natured demeanor, waddled over to Mary and Barkley. "If I may interject, ma'am," she said with a toothy grin. "It would be ever so delightful to host a royal garden party upon our return. A celebration of the new garden's completion."

Lady Mary's eyes lit with excitement and trepidation. "Cook, that's a marvelous idea! A garden party would be the perfect way to introduce our guests to the grandeur of the renovated estate. As long as we have the finances remaining for such an event."

Cook's face flushed with pride. "I'm glad you agree. Though, I wouldn't have the faintest, about the finances." Cook wiped her brow on her shirtsleeve. "I can already envision the lavish spread—delectable finger sandwiches, dainty pastries, and, of course, a selection of the finest teas." She squealed with delight and then clapped her hands. Mary chuckled, but Cook quickly regained her composure.

Barkley barked happily while hopping around in the tall grass, giving his approval.

Mary's mind raced with possibilities. "And we must invite the most notable guests and dignitaries. Lord and Lady Abernoothy, Sir Reginald Steal, and perhaps even the Duchess of Mothford."

"Reginald Steal was dabbling in the snuff business, last I heard," Cook added out of turn. She flashed a look of disgust before fixing her face with a pocket compact, a huge grin on her face.

With a stern squeal, the last bolt on the spare tire tightened, and Ponsonby murmured in agreement, "A gathering of esteemed people will undoubtedly set the tone for a day of sophisticated and genteel entertainment."

Cook clapped her hands one more time. "I'll prepare the meals for a garden party fit for royalty."

Mary resisted rolling her eyes at the woman's obviousness. Instead she clicked her tongue for Barkley to come to her side while Ponsonby finished with the tire.

Mary peered down the road for passing cars. Ponsonby

dusted off his hands. "We should be back on our way shortly, my lady."

She climbed back into the car, Barkley leaping in after her. The countryside was absent of other motor vehicles—and quiet save for the distant song of a skylark.

Cook settled herself, and Ponsonby slid into the driver's seat once more. Mary gazed between her loyal companions—Barkley, nose to the window; Ponsonby, who had finished his task with precision; and Cook, already planning menus in her head. Ponsonby steered the vintage car back onto the road as the engine's purr filled the air once more.

"We must invite Winnie, Dotty and Margie, and their parents of course—to thank them for a most unforgettable trip." A rueful smile curled Mary's lips as she settled into a comfortable position in her own seat. Barkley wagged his tail happily, but Mary furrowed her brow in contemplation. "Ponsonby, this is the second flat tire we've encountered. It's a blessing we don't have these quandaries at the Snodsbury estate. Though, it does make one wonder if there really *is* more happening in Upper Wainbury, after all."

READ ROYALLY SNUFFED

Leave a review!

Thank you for reading our book!
We appreciate your feedback and love to
hear about how you enjoyed it!

Please leave a positive review letting us
know what you thought.

DUCHESS OF SNODSBURY TRILOGY

From the creative writers: P.C. James, author of the Best-Selling Miss Riddell Cozy Mystery Series and Kathryn Mykel, Award-Winning author of Best-Selling Sewing Suspicion, Quilting Cozy Mystery.

Royally Dispatched Released in 2022
Royally Whacked Released in 2023
Royally Snuffed Coming in 2024

SASSY SENIOR SLEUTHS

Sassy Senior Sleuths

Sassy Senior Sleuths Return

Travel can be murder. Can Miss Riddell and Nona catch the villains before they become victims?

Travel forward from the Miss Riddell series to the twenty-first century with the demure Miss Pauline Riddell as she befriends a strangely lovable, fly by the seat of her pants amateur sleuth, named Gretta Galia aka Nona. The two sixty-five year-old travel companions visit tourist traps around the United States.

These stories move forward about twenty years from the Miss Riddell Series by P.C. James and back in time about twenty years from the Quilting Cozy Mystery series by Kathryn Mykel. Approximating the setting of these stories to be during the turn of the 21st century, between 2000-2005.

Join us in the Adventures of Pauline and Nona Facebook group and let us know you've read the story, what you think of this quick mini mystery; and if you made the recipe! https://www.facebook.com/groups/paulineandnona/

From the creative writers: P.C. James, author of the Best-Selling Miss Riddell Cozy Mystery Series and Kathryn Mykel, author of Award-Winning Quilting Cozy Mystery Series starting with Sewing Suspicion.

ABOUT THE AUTHOR KATHRYN MYKEL

Kathryn Mykel, author of Quilting Cozy Mysteries

Inspired by the laugh-out-loud and fanciful aspects of cozies, Kathryn aims to write lighthearted, humorous mysteries that play on her passion for the craft of quilting. She's an avid quilter, born and raised in a small New England town.

Website:
www.authorkathrynmykel.com

Facebook
https://www.facebook.com/AuthorKathrynMykel

Bookbub
https://www.bookbub.com/profile/kathryn-mykel

GoodReads
https://www.goodreads.com/author/show/21921434.Kathryn_Mykel

Award-winning author of best-selling quilting cozy mystery series:

Sewing Suspicion
2021 Indie Cozy Mystery Book of The Year
Quilting Calamity
2022 Indie Cozy Mystery Book of The Year

Quilting Cozy Mystery Series:
Sewing Suspicion (Book 1)
Quilting Calamity (Book 2)
Pressing Matters (Book 3)
Mutterly Mistaken
(Holiday Pet Sleuths Series) (Book 3.5)
Threading Trouble (Book 4)
Paw-in-Law
(Holiday Pet Sleuths Series) (Book 4.5)
Stitching Concerns (Book 5)
Purrfect Perpetrator
(Holiday Pet Sleuths Series) (Book 5.5)
Mending Mischief (Book 6)
Doggone Disaster
(Holiday Pet Sleuths Series) (Book 6.5)

Book Set 1
Includes Books (1-3):
Sewing Suspicion, Quilting Calamity & Pressing Matters

Book Set 2
Includes Books (1-5):
Sewing Suspicion, Quilting Calamity, Pressing Matters, Threading Trouble & Stitching Concerns

Cozy Mysteries by Kathryn Mykel & P.C. James:
Senior Sassy Sleuths Series
(Short Stories, Shared Main Characters)
Senior Sassy Sleuths
Senior Sassy Sleuths Return
Senior Sassy Sleuths on the Trail

Anthology Series
(Short stories by multiple authors)
A Cauldron of Deceptions
A Campsite of Culprits
A Vacation of Mischief
An Aquarium of Deceit
A Bookworm of A Suspect
A Festival of Forensics
A Haunting of Revenge
Little Shop of Murders

1950s Cozy Mysteries by
Kathryn Mykel & P.C. James:

Duchess of Snodsbury Mysteries
Royally Dispatched
Royally Whacked
Royally Snuffed

ABOUT THE AUTHOR P.C. JAMES

P.C. James, Author of the Miss Riddell Series

I've always loved mysteries, especially those involving Agatha Christie's Miss Marple so, after retiring, I became an author. Now I have a best-selling series, Miss Riddell's Cozy Mysteries, which keeps me busy. When I'm not feverishly typing on my laptop, you'll find me running, cycling, walking, and taking wildlife photos wherever and whenever I can.

Facebook
https://www.facebook.com/PCJamesAuthor

Bookbub
https://www.bookbub.com/authors/p-c-james

Amazon Author Page
https://www.amazon.com/P.-C.-James/e/B08VTN7Z8Y

GoodReads
https://www.goodreads.com/author/show/20856827.P_C_James

Amazon Series Page
Miss Riddell Cozy Mysteries

Miss Riddell Newsletter signup
https://landing.mailerlite.com/webforms/landing/x7a9e4

Books on Amazon:

<u>In the Beginning, There Was a Murder</u>
<u>Then There Were ... Two Murders?</u>
<u>The Past Never Dies</u>
<u>A Murder for Christmas</u>
<u>Miss Riddell and the Heiress</u>
<u>Miss Riddell's Paranormal Mystery</u>
<u>The Girl in the Gazebo</u>
<u>The Dead of Winter</u>
<u>It's Murder, on a Galapagos Cruise</u>
Miss Riddell and the Pet Thefts

One Man and His Dog Cozy Mysteries
Hey Diddle Diddle, the Runaway Riddle

Printed in Poland
by Amazon Fulfillment
Poland Sp. z o.o., Wrocław